'Original and thought-provoking' Live and Deadly

'Yet another brilliantly complex and superbly plotted crime thriller that I would highly recommend' Cal Turner Reviews

'Lilja is a brilliantly talented writer and I love her use of language, especially in her descriptions of the scenery' Bantam Bookworm

'Highly recommended to all readers who enjoy a well-executed crime thriller' Fictionophile

'Dark, mysterious, and certainly keeps you guessing all the way to the end' Monika Reads

'This series just gets better with every book!'
From Belgium with Book Love

'Loads of twists and turns but still a mystery at the end'
Sally Boocock

'It's dark, it's twisty, nothing is ever as it seems' Loopy Kaz

'An incredibly atmospheric world for these characters and their investigations' The Butler Did It

'Well written, it sent chills through me whilst reading!' Judefire33

'An atmospheric and dramatic storyline' Lynda's Book Reviews

ABOUT THE AUTHOR

Icelandic crime writer Lilja Sigurðardóttir was born in the town of Akranes in 1972 and raised in Mexico, Sweden, Spain and Iceland. An award-winning playwright, Lilja has written eleven crime novels, including *Snare*, *Trap* and *Cage*, making up the Reykjavík Noir trilogy, and her standalone thriller *Betrayal*, all of which have hit bestseller lists worldwide. *Snare* was longlisted for the CWA International Dagger, *Cage* won Best Icelandic Crime Novel of the Year and was a *Guardian* Book of the Year, and *Betrayal* was shortlisted for the prestigious Glass Key Award and won Icelandic Crime Novel of the Year. The film rights for the Reykjavík Noir trilogy have been bought by Glassriver. *Cold as Hell*, the first book in the An Áróra Investigation series, was published in the UK in 2021 and was followed by *Red as Blood, White as Snow* and *Dark as Night*. TV rights to the series have been bought by Studio Zentral in Germany.

Lilja lives in Reykjavík with her partner. You'll find her on X @LiljaWriter, Instagram @sigurdardottirlilja, on Facebook.com/liljawriter and on her website, liljawriter.com.

ABOUT THE TRANSLATOR

Lorenza Garcia spent her early adulthood living and working in Iceland, Spain and France. She has been a full-time literary translator since 2008 and has translated and co-translated over forty novels and works of non-fiction from French, Spanish and Icelandic. She currently lives in South London with her Tibetan Terrier.

BLACK AS DEATH

Lilja Sigurðardóttir

Translated by Lorenza Garcia

**ORENDA
BOOKS**

Orenda Books
16 Carson Road
West Dulwich
London SE21 8HU
www.orendabooks.co.uk

First published in Icelandic as *Dauðadjúp sprunga* by Forlagið, 2023
First published in English by Orenda Books, 2025
Copyright © Lilja Sigurðardóttir, 2023
English translation copyright © Lorenza Garcia, 2025

A catalogue record for this book is available from the British Library.

B-format paperback ISBN 978-1-916788-84-8
eISBN 978-1-916788-85-5

The publication of this translation has been made possible
through the financial support of

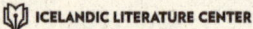

ICELANDIC LITERATURE CENTER

Typeset in Garamond by typesetter.org.uk

Printed and bound by Clays Ltd, Elcograf S.p.A

MIX
Paper | Supporting
responsible forestry
FSC® C018072

For sales and distribution, please contact *info@orendabooks.co.uk*

BLACK AS DEATH

PRONUNCIATION GUIDE

Icelandic has a couple of letters that don't exist in other European languages and which are not always easy to replicate. The letter ð is generally replaced with a *d* in English, but we have decided to use the Icelandic letter to remain closer to the original names. Its sound is closest to the voiced *th* in English, as found in *th*en and ba*th*e.

The Icelandic letter þ is reproduced as *th*, as in *Th*orleifur, and is equivalent to an unvoiced *th* in English, as in *th*ing or *th*ump.

The letter *r* is generally rolled hard with the tongue against the roof of the mouth.

In pronouncing Icelandic personal and place names, the emphasis is always placed on the first syllable.

Áróra – Ow-row-ra
Baldvin – Bal-dvin
Björn – Bjoern
Engihjalli – Eng-e-hjattly
Grímur – Gree-muhr
Gúgúlú – Gue-gue-lue
Hafnarfjörður – Hap-nar-fjeor- thur
Hringbraut – Hring-broyt
Hvolsvöllur – Kvols-vull-uhr
Ísafold – Eesa-fold
Keflavík – Kep-la-veek
Kristján – Krist-tyown
Lauganes – Lœga-ness
Laugardalur – Lœ-gar-dahlur
Laurus – Low-rus
Miklabraut – Mikla-broyt

Oddsteinn – Odd-stay-tn
Reykjanes – Rey-kjah-ness
Seltjarnarnes – Sell-tjar-nar- ness
Seyðisfjörður – Say-this-fjoer-thur
Síðumúli – seethu-mooli
Snæþór Ómar – Snie-thor Oh-mar
Sturla – Sturt-lah
Sæbraut – Sigh-broyt
Vatnajökull – Vat-n-a-yer-kootl

1

'You know what to do, Ísafold,' her sister Áróra would doubtless have said, and Ísafold could imagine the weariness in her voice. Áróra had always been so dogged, so ready to fight her sister's battles for her, but the last time Ísafold contacted her, it was obvious she had given up on her. 'Call the Women's Shelter,' Áróra had told her then, and Ísafold had whispered back: 'I know, I know. But I'm locked in the bathroom right now, and I don't know if he's gone to bed yet so I'm afraid to go out.'

And here she was, a few weeks later, in the same situation. She gave a sniff and dried her face on the towel. She didn't have a nose-bleed, at least. The towel would be red otherwise. Björn had punched her straight in the face, but the blow had caught her cheek. Then he'd grabbed her round the neck and squeezed hard. This time she came close to blacking out before he'd let go.

The bathroom window was open, but she didn't dare get up to close it; she felt safer where she was, sitting on the floor. The door was locked, however Björn would often kick it, and she was scared the lock might give way, so she sat with her back against it, feet braced against the tub. She was clasping her phone in her hand and staring at it. Áróra was the only person in the world she wanted to call. To confide in. The last time she did that, though, Áróra had told her to call the emergency services. Ísafold felt a wave of dread rise inside her and almost threw up.

'No,' she'd whispered then. 'He'll only be even angrier tomorrow.'

'You see!' Áróra had declared, with an air of triumph. 'You're already thinking about what will happen when you go back to him. How can I take seriously what you said just now, about being ready to leave him this time? Yet you expect me to fly over to Iceland to rescue you or ... or what? I don't even understand what it is you want me to do.'

'I don't either,' Ísafold had breathed into the phone, feeling her voice falter. It was only this sense of aloneness she'd felt the need to share with her sister. And she had that same feeling now. She needed to convey to someone she trusted how utterly alone a person is in the face of violence. How the pain of the blows almost pales in comparison to the aching loneliness that fills one's whole being. Yet she had never been able to convey this to Áróra, nor would she succeed now if she called her. Áróra was so sorted. Áróra was so strong. Áróra had no problem hitting back.

'How many times have I dropped everything to rush over to Iceland to try to help you?' Áróra had said that last time they'd spoken. 'Only for you to go back to him before the black eye he gave you has even healed.'

'I don't blame you for giving up on me,' Ísafold had whispered then, and her sister had sighed at the other end of the phone.

'I haven't given up on you, Ísafold,' Áróra replied wearily. 'I just can't be responsible for you anymore. You know your options and you can decide for yourself. If you don't want to involve the police you call your brother-in-law, Ebbi, and he'll come straight over to fetch you. You've been through it all before so you know the drill. I don't see what good I can do by rushing over to Iceland to hold your hand.'

If Ísafold called her sister now, Áróra would simply repeat the same thing. And she'd be justified. It was unfair of Ísafold to want to share her suffering with her sister. Áróra had the right to live her perfect life in peace, without Ísafold imposing her misery on her.

Ísafold dabbed her face again with the towel; the salty tears stung her cheek.

'I think,' she whispered into the silence, 'I think he'll end up killing me soon.'

MONDAY

2

The rain was bucketing down, so Felix sat in his car for a while, in the hope the downpour would stop, or at least subside a little before he ventured out. He turned on the radio breakfast news but couldn't concentrate. His mind was a blur and he felt dreadfully sleepy, having woken up earlier than usual to begin his rounds for Sturla before noon. This was because the previous afternoon he'd been unable to get hold of anybody; it was as if they'd conspired to make themselves scarce, so that, eventually, he'd given up and gone home.

It didn't look as though the rain would let up anytime soon. He'd have to brave the short distance between the car park and the apartment block and hope he didn't get drenched. He zipped up his jacket, turned his collar up and silently cursed himself for not having worn his usual hoodie; the rain would mess up his hair, which had taken him so long to fix that morning – getting the middle parting straight, arranging his fringe so it fell over his forehead just the way he liked. He took a deep breath, stepped out of the car and made a dash for it across the car park, slowing down only when he'd reached the passageway that led from the street to the apartment block. There, he shook himself as might a dog and stood still for a moment to allow his heart to calm down.

His first stop was the Hippy – an ageing, small-time dealer who'd been selling grass for years and had recently branched out into pills. Felix knocked on the man's door and had to wait a while before he came to open it. His long hair was dishevelled and his eyes looked bloodshot.

'Felix,' he murmured, handing him a bundle of notes. 'Tell Sturla I'll give him the rest next week, will you?'

Felix gave a nod, and a feeling of dread gripped his throat. He gave a little cough: 'You know Sturla doesn't like it when people are late with their payments.' He didn't need to tell the Hippy this; Sturla had a reputation for being a hard-ass, and his debtors could expect to pay with their blood. And not only his debtors, his debt collectors, too. Felix truly didn't look forward to passing the Hippy's message on to his boss.

His next stop was the Bartender. Felix arrived when the bar was being cleaned – chairs were upside down on the tables, and although the doors and windows had been flung wide open, the stench of stale beer seemed to have impregnated the paintwork, and the only effect of the detergent was to create a nauseating cocktail that made Felix want to retch. The Bartender instantly slid an envelope across the counter.

'It's all there, plus a bit extra to compensate for last week,' he said. 'Be sure to mention that to Sturla, will you?'

'I will,' Felix said, stuffing the envelope into his pocket. 'Consider yourself lucky Sturla didn't come here in person to collect what was owing.' The flash of fear he saw in the Bartender's eyes made him feel better. It was good they all knew Sturla was monitoring things. It made his job easier. He disliked having to beat people up.

3

'Any news about the investigation?' Áróra said, not really sure why she was asking. They had only planned to meet for lunch, as they sometimes did, but it had made Daníel so awkwardly happy that Áróra reproached herself for not taking the initiative to organise these treats more often.

'You know I can't discuss an ongoing case with you. Even if it does relate to your sister. Besides, I'm no longer part of the investigation. Gutti is in charge of it, as you well know, Áróra.'

'Still, you must be following their progress, keeping abreast of what's going on,' she said, and instantly regretted it. From the expression on Daníel's face, she realised she'd probably insisted too much. He assumed a faraway look, avoiding eye contact, and she could almost hear the mental drawbridge going up. But this wasn't only about not discussing the case with her. He knew something – something he hadn't yet told her.

'It has to go through the proper channels,' he said at last. 'Can't we just enjoy this delicious food?'

Áróra nodded, contemplating the plate of salad before her. It contained all her favourite ingredients – avocado, feta cheese, spinach, chickpeas, with a tasty dressing on top – but she wasn't hungry. Even though lunch had been her idea. The food hall at Hlemmur was their habitual meeting place: it was handy for Daníel to nip across the road from the station, and easy for them both to find the food that suited them. Áróra needed something light as she'd be heading to The Gym afterwards to lift weights, whereas Daníel seemed to have no trouble putting away two square meals a day.

'I'm sorry, Daníel,' she said, sliding her hand across the table. He clasped hold of it, squeezing it gently, then stroked the back of her hand with his thumb, sending a frisson of pleasure up her arm that spread through her whole body. She felt a flash of embarrassment and glanced at the tourists sitting at the nearby tables. Of course, no one was paying any attention. Why would anyone be interested in whether a couple held hands or not? She returned the gesture. 'I can't help feeling strange, knowing a whole team is over there looking into Ísafold's death, and I have no idea what's going on. We've waited four years, and now, at last, when the case has taken off again, it's hard not knowing whether they've found something new.'

'Anything new,' Daníel echoed, cutting in. 'Look, cold cases like this are always tricky, and—'

Now it was her turn to interrupt. 'There is something new. I can see it on your face, Daníel. I know you well enough by now to see when you're keeping something from me. And the longer you keep it from me, the more awkward things will get between us. Whenever I mention Ísafold's name you get that evasive look. I know you're hiding something from me.'

Daníel struggled for a moment to cut up the duck thigh on his plate, then shovelled two forkfuls into his mouth, chewing vigorously and with an air of irritation. Then he emptied his glass of water in one gulp and rose swiftly from his chair.

'All right,' he said.

'All right?' she repeated, not sure how to interpret this abrupt end to their meal.

'Let's cross the street and talk to Gutti. There's something he needs to tell you.'

4

Daníel checked his phone as they mounted the steps of the police station. There was nothing pressing, and he hoped it would stay that way so he could accompany Áróra when she spoke to Gutti.

He'd been dreading this moment for a few days, ever since, anxious for an update about the investigation, he'd dragged the information out of Gutti and Helena. At the same time, he was relieved, because he'd been forced to behave towards Áróra as if he knew nothing. But it hadn't worked. It never did. She always saw through him.

There was nowhere for them to sit downstairs, so they installed themselves in the nicer canteen on the top floor; it wouldn't matter if they took it over for a while as hardly anyone used it, and if somebody did decide to sneak in to use the good coffee machine they'd see through the windows in the corridor that an interview was taking place. Besides, it was cosier in there than in one of the bleak downstairs offices. The carpet tiles on the floor and one wall had the effect of softening any sounds, and the row of windows looking out onto Mount Esja offered the eyes, as well as the soul, a chance to find repose in its blue-green hues.

Daníel wasn't sure how Áróra would respond – only that she would take it badly. She'd either adopt a tough attitude, snap at them, and say they had no right to withhold such an important piece of information from her, in which case it would take him days to calm her down. Or she'd be depressed and hurt. This would undoubtedly be worse. He didn't know how to handle her when she retreated into herself.

After the discovery of her sister's body earlier that spring, the strength Áróra had previously shown became fragile, the shell she'd so carefully constructed around herself threatening to crack at any moment. Despite long claiming she had no hope of her sister being found alive, the finality of knowing had somehow amplified her pain. As if she'd been holding part of her grief at bay until her sister's death was confirmed. Until they found her body.

Daníel had just finished setting out the coffee cups when Gutti walked in and closed the door behind him. He shook his head when Daníel pointed inquiringly at the coffee machine, and sat down at the table opposite Áróra. Gutti wasn't carrying anything. Neither his phone nor a report file of the sort detective chief inspectors habitually clutch, as they might a safety rope. It was always possible to open such a file and flick through its contents if an interview got a bit awkward, as if they'd suddenly thought of something they had to check, when in fact they looked up any information they needed on the police database – LÖKE.

'Well, Áróra, my dear,' Gutti said, in a voice so benign he couldn't be criticised for employing a term of endearment that suggested a familiarity that didn't exist. Gutti had only been involved with the Ísafold case for a few weeks, and had struggled to get up to speed, both with the missing-person investigation, as well as the discovery of the body. The two bodies. And this was where Gutti decided to start. 'We have the remains of two individuals,' he said. 'Your sister, Ísafold, and her partner, Björn, and as you're aware this discovery entirely contradicts our initial theory that Björn killed Ísafold before fleeing to Canada.'

Áróra said nothing, simply nodded. Daníel contemplated her face, but couldn't read her thoughts. Her expression gave nothing away, other than that she was waiting expectantly. Waiting to hear what Gutti was about to tell her.

'I assume you know, through Daníel, how police investigations work,' he resumed.

But Áróra shook her head. 'Not really. Daníel and I haven't been together long enough for me to become any kind of expert on the subject.'

Gutti was slightly taken aback by her brusque response but quickly collected himself. 'Yes, no, no. Right.' He cleared his throat. 'What I ought to have said is that in cases like these we sometimes choose to withhold certain details. For a limited time, of course. These are often details that risk causing a stir in the sensationalist media, upsetting the victims' families, or elements we can use to verify the statements of people who claim to know something. Usually they relate to some characteristic, some peculiarity of the case, or in this instance...' Gutti sighed then drew a deep breath, making his shirt stretch over his ever more prominent beer belly '...about the victim. Your sister.'

'What?' Áróra was now staring straight at Gutti, who shot a sidelong glance at Daníel, as though hoping he might help him out.

He had no intention of doing any such thing; he would never have chosen to withhold this information from Áróra if he'd been leading the investigation. 'Tell her,' he said.

'Yes. Ahem.' Gutti gave another little cough, and glanced furtively at Áróra, as though afraid to look her in the eye. 'The result of the autopsy revealed an interesting ... or, how should I put it? ... a curious detail regarding Ísafold's body.'

'What?' Áróra repeated, only now her tone was different. Now she sounded scared. Hesitant. As though she wasn't sure she wanted to know more.

'Her heart was missing.'

'What?' Áróra shook her head in disbelief, as if Gutti's words hadn't registered. 'What do you mean?'

'Whoever killed Ísafold apparently ... Well. They removed her heart.'

Áróra made as if to speak, then turned her head slightly and gazed out of the window open-mouthed, the way a baby needing to rest its overstimulated senses might avert its eyes while it processes new experiences. Just then a big cloud scudded across the northern sky, casting a dark shadow over Esja.

Áróra turned once more to Gutti. 'What about Björn? Was his…?'

'No,' Gutti replied instantly. 'Björn was intact. I mean, none of his organs were missing. Only a few broken bones due to his body being crammed into the suitcase—'

'Too much information,' Daníel cut in, but Áróra shook her head.

'No. I want to know,' she said. 'I want to know everything.'

Gutti now looked her in the eye and nodded. 'I understand. But in fact, the information about the heart is the only detail we've kept to ourselves, because – how shall I put this? – it suggests a different type of murder than the ones we're used to dealing with here in Iceland. As we already told you and your mother, due to the multiple injuries her body presented the autopsy was unable to determine the precise cause of Ísafold's death, and this is the only additional piece of information. That her heart was missing.'

5

Áróra refrained from screaming until she and Daníel were outside, on the police station steps. The heavy traffic around Hlemmur and two buses accelerating mostly drowned out her cries.

'How could you keep this a secret from me?' she yelled, pushing him away when he made to embrace her. She did not want to cry. She did not want his pity. She was furious, seething with righteous indignation.

'I heard about it a few days ago and I asked Gutti to tell you...' he began, but she didn't want to listen to him. She didn't want to be softened by that calm voice of his that was so good at soothing her.

'Her heart, Daníel! Her heart!' she cried, unsure herself what she was trying to express, only that there was something particularly painful about her sister's heart having been ripped out. She wouldn't have given a damn about a missing kidney. That would've been different. But a person's heart was somehow so central to their being. The dwelling place of emotions. Life's metronome.

'Áróra, darling...' Daníel made another attempt to embrace her, but she pulled away, folding her arms across her chest, and he backed off again.

She swallowed the lump rising in her throat and gave a low growl to rekindle her anger. 'How could you let us bury my sister without her heart? How could you be so insensitive? What do you think Mum will say when she hears about this?' Áróra gave a gasp. 'She mustn't find out. It would destroy her.' She grabbed Daníel's arm. 'You mustn't tell her!'

Daníel looked at her, saddened. 'Your mum knows about it,' he said calmly. 'Gutti told her as soon as we found out.'

'What?' Áróra gazed at him in astonishment. 'What...? How...?' She didn't even know which question to ask first. Her mind was a jumble of senseless thoughts.

'Your mum didn't want us to tell you,' Daníel said. 'She didn't want you to suffer. And as Ísafold's closest relative it was her decision to make.'

Áróra felt a flash of annoyance towards her mother, before realising how silly that was. Only a moment ago, she had implored Daníel to spare her mother by withholding the same information from her.

'Your mum was convinced you'd get the bit between your teeth and refuse to bury her until we'd found her heart,' Daníel went on. 'She also felt you both needed some kind of closure. Time to say your farewells.'

Áróra stared at him and a sense of unease crept over her. This wasn't over. This was far from being over. Not only had they yet to find Ísafold's killer. They also had to find part of her body. Ísafold wasn't whole where she lay buried in the ground next to their father.

'And ... and, what? Now you're looking for her heart?'

'I think that has to be in the mix, yes,' Daníel said. 'Although our decision to bury Ísafold's body as it was found, in consultation with your mum, was based on the fact that we may never find her heart.'

'How can you know that?' Áróra was shouting again.

'We can't,' Daníel replied calmly. 'We'll have to wait and see whether any clues emerge in the course of the investigation. This is still a cold case, even though it's only been a few weeks since we found the bodies.'

'Six weeks ago,' she said. 'You found them six weeks ago.'

'Yes,' Daníel replied softly, looking at her in a way that told her he was trying to read her thoughts.

'Stop it,' she said.

'Stop what?' he asked.

'Looking at me like that.'

He averted his eyes, and she wanted to shake him. She wanted to go on being angry, to shout and scold him, but she couldn't. She'd never been able to stay angry with him for long.

'Shall I drop you off at home, so you can rest for a while, collect yourself?' Daníel asked.

But Áróra shook her head. 'No,' she replied, and strode off. 'I'm going to The Gym to lift a hundred kilos.'

Ísafold gasped for breath on her way up the stairs, and felt her heart pounding in her chest. It wasn't due to the physical effort of walking up one floor but because the fear she felt had sent her entire body into a panic. She'd bedded down in the bathroom that night, rolling up a towel for a pillow and spreading her bathrobe over her. This had enabled her to drop off at intervals, when the pain didn't waken her, or some rustling sound startle her. Björn, on the other hand, seemed to have gone out like a light, and she hadn't heard him stir all night. So, at about eight in the morning, she had cautiously unlocked the bathroom door, and crept out without making a sound. Hearing Björn's snores coming from the front room, she counted her blessings, as it meant she could sneak into the bedroom to fetch some clothes. Turtleneck tops had become an essential item of clothing, and she had bought several in different colours with necks high enough to conceal finger marks or love bites. Depending on the circumstances.

She'd managed to slip out without waking Björn, and as work had been busy that day, she'd had plenty of other things to occupy her – a good many customers as well as a delivery that needed to be unloaded, inventoried and the clothes put on display. But now, as she forced herself to mount the stairs, one by one, panting like a pack animal, she was gripped with fear. If Björn was still drinking and seemed irritable, the best thing would be for her to turn around and try to leave straight away. Maybe she could stay with Björn's brother, Ebbi, or find a cheap hotel for the night. When Björn was like this, his bad mood usually lasted until he stopped drinking, then as the alcohol wore off his anger subsided.

She turned the key in the lock and walked calmly inside.

The radio was on in the kitchen and she could hear the clatter of pans.

'Hi, sweetheart,' Björn called as he peered out, a cheerful look on his face, as if yesterday evening had simply been a bad nightmare that had only taken place in her head.

'Hi?' She heard the questioning tone in her own greeting, as if she was testing his mood with her tentative hi. To see whether it was safe for her to be there.

'I'm cooking lasagne,' he called out, and she heaved a sigh. It seemed everything would be all right. Björn was no doubt hungover, and while that state lasted, he was often affectionate. It was safe for her to go in. She slipped off her parka and placed it on a hanger, then hooked her handbag round the neck of the hanger, which she always did, so she could grab what she needed in the event she had to flee. She walked slowly into the kitchen and was relieved to see Björn sipping a can of Coke while he cooked. 'I was thinking maybe we could rent a movie and eat our dinner in front of the TV,' he said, and for an instant Ísafold doubted whether yesterday evening had been as bad as she remembered. Had she blown what happened out of all proportion in her mind? Had Björn really tried to strangle her?

'Don't we need to talk first?' she asked softly, and he sighed.

'Yeah,' he said. 'Of course. I promise, no more booze in the near future.'

'It's not just that, Björn,' she said. 'You were so awful yesterday. I was terrified of you.' She felt her pulse quicken. There, she'd said it now, and she hardly dared breathe for fear of how he might react. But he didn't go crazy, nor did he laugh. He simply stared at her, with a look that suggested she'd said something hurtful. Then he walked up to her, and she recoiled instinctively, even though he seemed on the brink of tears. He stretched out his hand and drew her to him.

'Sweetheart,' he whispered, placing his arms about her.

It took Ísafold a while to relax in his embrace, to allow him to clasp her body against his, pull down the neck of her top and kiss her throat.

'Forgive me,' he whispered. 'I don't know what the hell's wrong with me. I love you so much.' His voice was quaking, his breath ragged, as if he were sobbing.

He sounded sincere, and Ísafold felt her defences melt away. Maybe yesterday had been bad enough to bring him to his senses? Maybe everything would be okay?

Áróra had almost reached The Gym when she decided to turn around and drive up to Kópavogur instead. Her heart was pounding so fast that the curious notion occurred to her that somehow it was beating for both her and Ísafold, and if she put too much strain on it, it would simply burst.

She felt she needed a foothold, some solid foundation to stand on, because earlier at the police station it was as if the rug had been pulled out from under her feet. As if everything she'd so far concluded about Ísafold's disappearance and death had been wrong, and something quite different had happened from what both she and the police had believed.

The block on Engihjalli towered above Áróra as she crossed the car park on her way to the entrance. The cluster of blocks perched on the crest of the hill like lighthouses, offering splendid views to residents whose apartments faced the right way. Björn and Ísafold's apartment didn't. It overlooked an industrial estate, with the blue sign of a builder's merchant in the foreground. Ísafold had always maintained she was living her dream life, which Áróra found strange, because for her the good life had a completely different meaning. But Ísafold insisted her dream had always been to live in Iceland, speak the language again, as well as she had when she was a kid, and adopt the Icelandic way of life. Áróra had never experienced this powerful need to feel connected to Iceland. Not until her sister disappeared.

The tower block seemed to trap the wind and funnel it downward, so Áróra found herself standing in a cold draught. She shivered, pulled her coat about her and pressed Olga's buzzer. Olga was a fellow resident in the block who had been kind to Ísafold, and was apparently one of the few of her and Björn's neighbours who still lived there. Áróra pressed the buzzer again, but no one replied. She was probably still at work. As she pressed the buzzer a third time, she heard a noise in the stairwell and saw through the glass that someone was coming down.

The door opened slowly and Áróra found herself face to face with Grímur, the other neighbour of Ísafold's she knew. Apparently, he'd come down to fetch his post and was surprised to see Áróra there.

'You're so like her,' was the first thing he said, and Áróra smiled. She'd always found Grímur strange. Felt a bit sorry for him. He seemed to suffer from some skin disease, as he was completely bald with no eyebrows, and his skin was red and puffy. More than once, however, when Björn went berserk, he'd helped Ísafold, and Ísafold had always referred to Grímur as her friend.

'How are you?' Áróra asked, and Grímur opened his mouth, hesitated then stammered:

'Not so bad.'

He didn't ask her anything in return, simply stood and looked searchingly at Áróra until she explained she'd been trying Olga's buzzer.

'Olga's not here at the moment, she's on holiday in Canada,' he said.

'Canada?' she repeated, and for an instant it was as if her thoughts came to a halt when confronted with this fact, and became stuck in some rut that wouldn't let her advance.

'Is there a particular reason why you wanted to see her?' Grímur asked, jolting Áróra's thoughts back into motion.

'No,' she replied. 'Nothing special. Just to have a chat with her, ask her if she remembered anything else about Ísafold.' Gutti had insisted she keep quiet about new information relating to the case. She mustn't tell a soul about this thing with the heart. So, she prevaricated. 'Now the investigation is back on track, I felt I had to do something. Be connected with the case in some way.'

'They've resumed the investigation?' Grímur seemed surprised.

'Yes. You know they found my sister's body?' she said. 'Both their bodies.'

'Indeed. Altogether very strange,' he said. 'Putting them in suitcases like that.'

Áróra nodded, and, not wishing to think about suitcases, about bodies stuffed into suitcases, she added: 'Well, then,' and made as if to leave. But then she remembered something else. 'Do you know who's living there now – in their old apartment?' She indicated the slot next to the buzzer, from which the card with her sister's and Björn's names had been removed.

'It's empty, has been ever since,' Grímur said.

'Really?' Áróra found this odd.

'Yes,' said Grímur. 'Björn's family only just cleared the apartment. They plan to put it up for sale. I gather it's a lengthy process to have a missing person pronounced dead. And for a long time Björn's mother believed her son would come back, so she held on to the place.'

'I see.' For the first time Áróra's felt sympathy for Björn's mother. In reality, she'd been in the same position as Áróra and her mother – suspended in uncertainty. Áróra had long condemned her for not having helped Ísafold. For refusing to acknowledge her son's violent character.

'I have the key if you want,' Grímur said then. 'Ísafold gave it to me once, and I kept it. So, if you want to go inside and take a look around, this could be your last chance before someone moves in.'

Áróra followed Grímur back up the stairs to his apartment where he slipped through the half-open door, indicating that he wanted her to remain outside while he fetched the key. Then she followed him up to the floor above and waited while he struggled to insert the key into the lock, his hand trembling. He stepped aside to let her go in first then entered the empty apartment behind her. They both came to a halt in the living room and stood silently for a while. For an instant, Áróra felt as if she had some connection with Ísafold, as if this room that had remained closed to the outside world for so long retained in its dusty walls some clue to her sister's final days.

The sensation quickly evaporated, and Áróra walked over to the window and looked out at the timber yard of the builder's merchant. Then, for some reason, she recalled what had made her thoughts stall just now. Canada.

8

Daniel frowned and rubbed his forehead. A drowsy feeling crept over him as he sat facing Ari Benz Liu, chief superintendent at the International Department of the Police Commissioner's Office, listening to him ramble on, the way he always did when he couldn't, or wouldn't, be straight with someone.

'This is a collaborative project,' Ari said. 'So, obviously, when Europol asks us for information, we comply.'

Daniel nodded glumly. 'Yet when it comes to explaining why they want the information they aren't forthcoming,' he retorted.

Ari grinned. 'No. They're the big chiefs. What I can tell you, off the record, is that I think it's linked to a big international money-laundering operation.'

Daniel heaved a sigh. He doubted he could wriggle out of this one, but he'd give it his best shot.

'You know how much financial crime bores me,' he muttered, and Ari laughed out loud, as if to make light of the whole matter.

'You can't have a murder every day,' he said with a smile. 'Besides, your boss tells me you're available. And, of course, your partner being an expert on financial crime makes you the perfect candidate. Come on, Daniel. We're talking two or three days here. By the weekend you'll probably have some brand-new violent crime to investigate. But until then, please do me this one favour!' Ari pouted and made puppy eyes at Daniel, who burst out laughing.

'Is that the face you use on women?' he said, but Ari shook his head.

'No,' he replied. 'I show them my sports car and they pounce on me like wild animals.'

Daniel found Ari amusing. He made sure he was the stereotype of an old-school bachelor. Lately, he'd had a different woman on his arm every few weeks, and had twice invited Daníel and Áróra on a double date. On both occasions, Daníel had felt like a caveman in comparison to Ari, who opened doors, pulled out chairs and helped women on with their coats, all the while showering them with compliments.

'Okay,' said Daníel. 'I'll look into it. What's the coffeehouse called?'

'Coffeehouses,' Ari corrected him. 'It's a chain. Kaffikó Ltd. They have branches all over town.'

Daníel raised his eyebrows. He knew Kaffikó well. After a few of them installed drive-thru hatches he would use them when he needed to grab a coffee on the hoof.

'What exactly is this company suspected of doing?' he asked.

Ari leaned back in his chair and threw up his hands. 'I can't give you any details, primarily because I don't know, but I expect the company's name popped up on some chatline monitored by Europol, and they want us to check out whether it's worth looking into.'

'In other words, it's nothing at all?'

'Most likely,' said Ari Benz. Daníel sighed. It was shaping up to be a fun week – or not.

'I'll look into it tomorrow,' he said rising from his chair.

'I owe you one, my friend,' Ari called after him. 'Beer, pizza, you name it!'

'You can lend me your car for a day,' Daníel called back. Then laughed at Ari's instant retort:

'No!'

9

'When Ísafold went missing, it was first assumed that she'd disappeared intentionally, because her partner was violent. Most people thought she'd simply had enough and left.' Helena tried to sound cheerful as she spoke to the young trainee police officer sitting next to her in the passenger seat. In fact, she was furious. This was the first task Gutti had assigned to her that wasn't trawling through endless security-camera footage, and she knew he'd only sent her to interview a witness because nobody else wanted to babysit the rookie. Her name was Vala and part of her on-the-job training was to observe a witness being interviewed. Vala was a twenty-five-year-old graduate from the police academy who had spent a few summers in uniform and was currently doing a masters in policing studies and aiming to work in CID. Helena thought she could smell the young woman's ambition, and it made her feel slightly uneasy. Or maybe her unease had more to do with the fact that Vala was stunningly attractive. Dangerously so, as Gutti had put it when he told the team in no uncertain terms that he didn't want any fucking MeToo stuff here. All the men had taken this as a warning to avoid Vala – as they might a naked flame. And so it was decided that Helena would be lumbered with the rookie, with all the headaches that entailed.

'But when the boyfriend also disappeared, this guy...' Vala said, opening her notebook and flipping through it eagerly.

'Björn,' Helena cut in. They had reached the Sæbraut bypass. On their way out, they'd bumped into some of the lads in traffic, who advised them to avoid lower Breiðhólt and Miklabraut, due to the roadworks popping up all over the city like a fuming, foul-smelling harbinger of spring, so Helena had decided to stay on the bypass. 'Áróra, Ísafold's sister, came over to Iceland to inquire about her, but soon after she arrived and starting asking around, Björn disappeared too. He was last seen walking out of Toronto Airport, before vanishing into thin air. The conclusion we drew from this was that Björn had killed Ísafold and then fled the law. Evidence found both in the apartment and in Björn's car suggested foul play, but then earlier this spring both his and Ísafold's bodies were found in suitcases inside a fissure on the Reykjanes peninsula.'

'And that was a game-changer,' Vala said, gazing thoughtfully out of the window.

Vala was pretty. So pretty that whenever Helena looked at her, she found herself staring. It was difficult not to. She had high cheekbones, long eyelashes, and her lips were so plump Helena wondered whether she'd had filler put in them. Yet she didn't seem the type who would go in for that sort of thing. On the contrary, she gave the impression of being sensible and down-to-earth, in her jeans and a cotton T-shirt, and she didn't wear make-up to work.

'Yes, it was a game-changer,' she replied, 'because a missing-person case turned into a murder investigation, and all our theories about what had happened went up in smoke.'

As they sped past Lauganes, Helena had a sudden urge to turn off to Laugardalur and check on Sirra. Say hi, see what she was up to. But that wasn't possible with the rookie tagging along. Not that she was in the habit of popping home while on duty. Sirra worked remotely and organised her own time, so Helena would occasionally call her around midday. Just for a chat. To discuss what they should have for supper or whisper sweet nothings to each other. But with the rookie by her side she couldn't make a personal call either.

For a moment an awkward silence filled the car. Helena was about to ask how Vala's studies were going, as if she were addressing a twelve-year-old, but thankfully Vala broke the silence before she managed to make a fool of herself.

'It's Olga and Grímur we have to talk to,' Vala said, checking the file.

'Neighbours in the block,' replied Helena. 'But it's just a follow-up.'

Follow-up had a good ring to it. It sounded authentic. She wasn't about to tell the rookie that in fact they'd been sent on an errand nobody else wanted. Namely, to question Olga for the umpteenth time about the chronology of events, or ask her to confirm what she'd said in her last interview, and the one prior to that; also to ask Grímur whether he might have seen such and such a vehicle parked outside the block, or if he recalled anything new. A series of box-ticking questions that were utterly pointless and would lead nowhere.

'Olga lives on the same floor as Ísafold and Björn and knew them well,' she went on. 'Chatted with them in the corridor, that sort of thing. Grímur, on the other hand, lives in the apartment right underneath theirs, so it seems he was more aware of the domestic abuse, as the noise obviously travelled downward.'

'Have you met them both before?' Vala asked.

Helena had to stifle her irritation. 'I've met them two or three times. I also did the follow-ups back then,' she said. 'After Ísafold and Björn disappeared.'

At Engihjalli, Helena parked in the lot furthest from the block and stepped out of the car. It was pointless getting irritated over having to carry out box-ticking exercises. With Gutti in charge, she realised she wouldn't be allotted any important assignments; at least this was preferable to being stuck behind a desk back at the station, and it was good to stretch her legs, even if she was lumbered with the rookie.

As they walked side by side towards the block, Helena showed Vala where Björn's car had been parked, and told her about the evidence inside the boot that suggested Ísafold had almost certainly been in there. Minute traces of blood and urine. Vala stopped in her tracks and looked about. She glanced up at the surrounding blocks and then at the car park.

'So a man lugged a big suitcase out to his car and stuffed it in his boot, and nobody thought anything of it?' she asked, and Helena nodded.

'That's the problem. Because the suitcase must have been heavy.'

Outside the block, Helena was poised to press the buzzer to Olga's apartment when the main door swung open. It took Helena a few seconds to connect the person coming out with the location.

'Áróra?' she said. 'What are you doing here?'

'I just dropped by to have a chat with my sister's neighbour,' Áróra replied. 'Only Olga isn't at home. She's on holiday in Canada. Don't you find it odd the number of times Canada has come up in this investigation?'

Sturla sat in his leather chair in the middle of the living room and eyed Felix coldly. It was as if he already knew there'd be money missing from today's collection. He had a sixth sense for these things. He cut a relaxed figure, dressed in chinos, his long legs stretched out in front of him, but his eyes told a different story.

'Felix,' he said, in a tone befitting a stern schoolteacher, and Felix felt a shiver go down his spine. 'Did everyone cough up?' Felix handed him the bundle of notes along with a slip of paper.

'Yes, they all paid something,' he said, praying Sturla wouldn't notice the tremor in his voice. 'Two of them are having a bit of trouble, though, and need a little more time.'

Sturla's gaze hardened even more. 'Time? Time is a luxury, Felix my boy; a luxury we cannot afford in our line of business. Any sign of weakness leaves us open to abuse, and I won't tolerate that.'

Felix swallowed hard. His throat was dry with fear, yet he managed to utter a reply. 'I get it,' he said. 'But maybe if we cut them some slack, they'll get back on their feet. For example, you gave the Barman a chance last week, and today he paid up, with interest.'

Sturla narrowed his eyes and gritted his teeth, making his jaw muscles ripple beneath the skin. Sturla hadn't given the Barman a chance – Felix had, and then he'd convinced Sturla it was fine.

'Giving people a chance is plain weakness, Felix. It encourages disobedience, and that gradually undermines our business. The only exception I make is when the police confiscate the goods.' He contemplated the slip of paper with the totals. 'These two guys who still owe me money need to cough up next time, with interest, otherwise they can expect a visit from me and the lads. Understood?'

Felix wanted to protest, but he knew it was risky to question Sturla's authority. He was already skating on thin ice.

'Understood,' he said. 'I'll make sure they pay up next time, with interest.'

Sturla continued to hold Felix's gaze, then his expression softened and he adopted the fatherly manner, which Felix wasn't sure he preferred over his toughness.

'You're such a talented guy, Felix,' Sturla said. 'Don't waste your talent by being sentimental. Never lose sight of who you're working for and what's at stake.'

Felix didn't need telling. Sturla, and his fear of Sturla, were never far from his thoughts – even in sleep, for he dreamed about the man. The quality of life he enjoyed thanks to the work he did for Sturla also served as a reminder not to rub his boss up the wrong way. Sturla paid him more than three times what he could earn on a building site, and Felix had happily gone to work for him after Björn disappeared. Despite having no illusions about the sort of person Sturla was – what he was capable of – he had willingly walked into the man's clutches. Even so, he was surprised at how much inner resistance he felt to Sturla's demands that he put the squeeze on the small-time dealers. Maybe Sturla was right: he was sentimental. And he'd do well to rein himself in, because Sturla wouldn't tolerate any rebelliousness or incompetence. And Felix had no intention of ending up like Björn.

11

For three days now Björn had been so nice to Ísafold that she'd begun to suspect something wasn't quite right. She was accustomed to the roses, the cooked meals, the kisses and cuddles, the sex – which was usually better the harsher the beating that preceded it, as if somehow the love was supposed to even out the hatred. But this was completely new. They hadn't made love since that dreadful evening, but Björn had been gentle and kind in a way that wasn't overbearing yet which she didn't recognise – and she couldn't appreciate. The whole thing felt so alien, as if he were singing a song he knew well purposely out of tune. He was being too nice, she had told Grímur, her downstairs neighbour, who stopped to ask how she was when they crossed in the hallway. Obviously, he'd noticed the noise the other night. Grímur had replied that surely this was a good thing. But she hadn't meant it like that. Of course, it was good that Björn was being nice to her; what was difficult to explain was her vague suspicion that he had some ulterior motive.

Something had shifted and she didn't know why or when that shift had occurred. Björn's current behaviour wasn't the result of genuine remorse – missing were the passion and tenderness, the thoughtfulness he showed her at the start of their relationship. Now it was as if he was pretending. Pretending he was sorry for beating her up. As if the frozen core inside him hadn't melted, hadn't softened when they made up. And if she was honest with herself, that was the problem. Björn was just pretending. He was hatching some plan, waiting for the right moment to put it into action.

Ísafold had been watching Björn closely, trying to interpret his expressions, his gestures, to the point where she felt like a gigantic nerve cell registering his every response. But it wasn't enough. She could never really see what he was thinking. She knew he was *cooking up something that involved her, she just didn't know what. Only that it was something awful.*

Björn had prepared breakfast, lunch and dinner for her three days in a row, carefully plating up her food and saying 'bon appetit' in French, as if serving up gastronomic delights were his greatest joy in life when in fact he loathed cooking.

'Thanks,' she said, forcing a smile. 'It looks yummy.' She stuck her fork into the latest fish supper he'd prepared and lifted it to her mouth – it did taste delicious.

'You deserve a bit of pampering,' he said, winking at her. He poured her a glass of white wine, while sticking to plain water himself, and for an instant Ísafold found herself wishing Björn would neck the rest of the bottle, followed by another, give her a beating and get it over with. It was too nerve-wracking waiting to find out what he was hiding behind this mask. What plan he really had in store for her.

She knew it was only a matter of time before he dropped the nice-guy act, but waiting was becoming unbearable.

At last the door opened a crack and Grímur peered out. When Helena saw the way Vala stared at him, she regretted not having warned her about Grímur's unusual appearance. He was, of course, as bald as last time, and the lack of any eyebrows gave his face a childlike look, despite his broad, masculine jaw. In addition, he had red scratches all over his cheeks and chin, as if he'd been a bit heavy-handed with the razor.

'Hello, Grímur,' Helena said amiably, and he shifted on his feet, seemingly unsure what to do next. 'We need to have a quick chat with you,' she went on. 'Perhaps you'd like to invite us in?'

Grímur gave a start, as if the obvious polite response had only just dawned on him, and he pulled open the door.

Before they knew it, she and Vala were sitting side by side on the rose-pattern sofa that must have either been a family heirloom, or from some charity shop. Helena had already decided that if Grímur offered them a coffee they'd accept. It would give them a pretext to stay longer, and people tended to speak more freely with a cup of coffee in their hand. However, Grímur didn't offer them anything. He sat stiffly in an armchair on the other side of the low table, and stared at them with an expression somewhere between curiosity and anguish.

'Is there any news on the Ísafold case?' he asked. 'Her sister Áróra just left – she told me the investigation was in full swing.'

Helena nodded. 'Yes, we bumped into Áróra, and she's right. The investigation into Ísafold's disappearance is now a murder case. A double murder case.' Helena wasn't sure but she thought she saw Grímur flinch.

'Yes, of course,' he said. 'Of course it's a double murder case. I gather Björn was found with her?'

'That's right,' Helena said. 'Both bodies were in the same fissure on the Reykjanes peninsula.' She cleared her throat and sat up straight. 'We want to know if you have anything to add to your original statement.' Out of the corner of her eye, Helena saw Vala open the case file and begin to read something. No doubt a summary of Grímur's testimony taken from previous interviews with him.

'No,' said Grímur. 'I don't recall anything else. Everything I have to say is in there,' he said, pointing at the file. Helena wondered whether his clipped responses were because he'd forgotten what he'd said previously, or simply that their visit made him uneasy. A lot of people found it awkward talking to the police, and Grímur struck her as the type who disliked interacting with people in general.

'How well did you know Ísafold and Björn?' she asked.

'Not very well,' Grímur replied. 'Ísafold and I knew each other to talk to. But I don't think I ever spoke to Björn. He wasn't the most courteous of men, he barely nodded at me in the hallway.'

Helena heard Vala tap a few times on the file, and she glanced at where her finger was resting on the text, next to Grímur's account of a conversation he'd had with Björn in which he mentioned he was going abroad.

'You don't recall discussing anything with him out in the hallway, the way neighbours chat to each other sometimes?'

'I'm not in the habit of poking my nose into other people's business,' he replied. 'And judging by the noises I heard coming from upstairs when he was beating her up, Björn wasn't a man I had any wish to get acquainted with.'

As Helena listened to Grímur, she reflected on how accurate people's memories were. It was perfectly understandable that a few trivial details might change over time, as the mind reassessed events, reinterpreted them in the light of information from other sources. Most people, however, tended to embroider rather than abbreviate. No matter how much time elapsed between interviews, it was rare for someone to forget an event that had actually taken place. And this troubled her. Contemplating Grímur as she got to her feet and said goodbye, Helena could sense he was relieved the interview was over. Vala took her leave of him too, with a dazzling smile that remained fixed on her lips until they were sitting outside in the car.

'Why in heaven's name didn't you ask him about the discrepancy in his statements?' she said.

'Precisely because his account differs so wildly from what he said originally,' Helena replied. 'We'll visit him again tomorrow and continue questioning him.'

'Why tomorrow; why not now?' asked Vala.

'You saw how stressed he was,' Helena replied. 'Well, he'll be twice as stressed when we go back tomorrow. One visit is routine; two means you're a person of interest. Grímur isn't a man who can cope very well with that, which will work to our advantage.'

Vala looked at Helena and grinned. 'I've learned something really useful today,' she said, seemingly contented.

Helena was contented, too. The irritation she'd felt earlier had vanished, and she felt her heart leap with joy. She was excited in that way she always was when something new emerged in a case. She sensed that if she put just a little more pressure on Grímur a fresh lead would open up. Truth was like water. It would always find a crack in someone's story and seep through.

Áróra didn't lift a hundred kilos at The Gym, as she'd told Daníel she would. Still, by the time she had finished her training session, she'd probably lifted over a thousand kilos in total and was drenched in sweat. She'd practised more fast reps than usual but with less weight, the aim being to let off more steam. And now she was exhausted and barely had the strength to pick up her phone, which was stubbornly ringing on the floor beside the bench press. As she reached for it, she resolved to refuse the call if it was Daníel. She needed to compose herself better before speaking to him.

Yet somehow it was as if her body overruled her mind and before she knew it, she'd sat up and taken the call.

'Áróra,' Daníel said softly.

'Hm,' Áróra responded. Her jaw was clenched, but not from the tension of lifting weights. It was as if her body, unbidden, were contriving to help her hold back the tears. If she relaxed, she'd cry. And she was afraid that if she started she wouldn't be able to stop.

'Shall we have a little talk?' he asked in a low voice, so low it was almost a whisper. And then she made out the distinctive warm, deep tone that usually softened her.

'No,' hissed Áróra and hung up.

She climbed into the shower cubicle screened off by a white plastic partition at the far end of The Gym, and turned on the tap. She undressed, tossed her clothes in a pile on the floor, and gasped as she stepped under the ice-cold shower. She didn't know why they'd never installed hot water. Maybe to deter people from hogging the shower, or because it was simpler to attach a shower head to the pipe in what had been a double garage, before it was converted into a weight-lifting room. And now it had become the custom, an essential part of the strong-man culture that presided in The Gym, to take a cold shower after training. As Áróra was the only woman there, she always did her best not to let out a shriek when she stepped under the ice-cold water, because any yells coming from the shower were invariably greeted by a hail of laughter from the men who were training.

Drying herself off rapidly, she pulled on her jeans and T-shirt, her body still burning, although the cold water had stopped her from sweating and had cleared her thoughts a little. At least she no longer felt on the brink of tears. On her way out she waved to a giant with a flowing beard attempting to deadlift 150 kilos, and was halfway across the yard when her phone rang again.

It was Daníel. Again.

'I just spoke to Helena,' he said.

'Really,' Áróra replied brusquely, biting her tongue to stifle the urge she felt to yell at him.

'She told me you've been speaking to a witness,' he said.

'I wasn't speaking to a witness,' she snapped. 'I had a chat with a friend of my sister's. One of the few friends she had towards the end.'

'I have one more interview to do,' said Daníel. 'Then shall we meet? We could go for dinner somewhere.'

'No,' said Áróra. She didn't want to see him right now. She would only start crying, and she couldn't allow herself to open up that never-ending wellspring.

14

The sound of alarm in Sirra's voice tied Helena's stomach in knots. There was an urgency in her tone, and Helena recognised the subtle tremor, like a taut string resonating just outside the scope of what she was saying.

'You need to come home,' she said. 'Right now.'

'What's the matter, Sirra?' Helena asked, and out of the corner of her eye saw Vala look at her searchingly. They hadn't spoken much since leaving Kópavogur, only to exchange a few comments about the case and Grímur's strangeness, but otherwise Vala had her head buried in the case file, and Helena was focused on driving.

'Immigration,' Sirra whispered. 'Someone has made a complaint about us.'

Helena performed an illegal U-turn on Suðurlandsbraut, took a left and drove as fast as was, in her estimation, reasonably acceptable along Laugardalur Valley.

'What's going on?' Vala asked.

Helena murmured something about having to stop off briefly at her house. There was a bit of an emergency. She ignored all further questions, except to say no when Vala asked whether someone had been injured, taken ill or was having their car towed away. It seemed this was the extent of a police officer's imagination; it would have taken a particularly lively one to envisage Helena, Sirra and Bisi's domestic arrangement.

The tyres screeched as Helena turned into the driveway at the house and, jerking on the handbrake, brought the car to a halt next to the police vehicle already parked there.

'Wait here!' she barked at Vala, as she leapt out and charged up the steps.

Helena strode through the open front door and headed towards the voices coming from the living room. A woman in a skirt suit towered over Bisi, who sat hunched on the sofa next to a uniformed police officer. Sirra stood facing the woman in a suit, arms folded across her chest, and on her face a resolute look that Helena had thankfully seldom seen.

'So, this is the third one?' the woman said, eyeing Helena from head to toe as she entered the room. The question seemed directed at no one in particular, and remained hanging in the air for anyone to answer.

'Yes, I'm the third resident here. My name's Helena.' She walked up to the woman and extended her hand. 'I rent the front room from Sirra and Bisi. They were kind enough to offer it to me while I have some work done on my apartment. What's the problem, and what is this about?'

'We received a tip-off that the situation here isn't quite what it seems,' the woman said. 'That you might be breaching immigration rules.'

'That's strange,' Helena said, pulling out her police badge and waving it in the air. 'As a police officer I would never encourage or turn a blind eye to any lawbreaking. Except for the food Bisi cooks, which is so spicy it should probably be made illegal.'

The woman forced a bitter smile.

'Is everything all right?' They looked as one at Vala, who was standing in the doorway, contemplating this curious gathering.

'Everything's fine. It's good you're here,' Helena said. 'May I introduce Vala, who is taking a masters in policing studies. Funnily enough, her main thesis is on institutional racism and homophobia.'

15

Daníel was tightening the hinges on the garden gate when he heard a clatter of heels behind him. He thought he recognised that stride and swung round. It was as he'd suspected. None other than Lady Gúgúlú was sailing swiftly towards him, in full drag, a pale-blue, mid-thigh-length, wispy dress, a wig the size of a small haystack and embroidered cowboy boots with steel heel taps that clacked on the pavement. She had a suitcase in one hand and in the other a Bónus shopping bag bursting at the seams.

'Daníel, darling!' she cried, and Daníel smiled and spread his arms.

'*Rara avis!*' he exclaimed.

'Peacock, darling, if you insist on comparing me to a bird. Peacock.' Lady handed Daníel her baggage, 'I assume my apartment's still for rent?'

'Yes, but—' This was as far as Daníel got.

'Good. I'll need a mattress, though, because my furniture was stolen.'

Daníel chuckled. Arguably it was a mild understatement to describe the events earlier that spring as having her furniture stolen, but that was typical of Lady. She was equally capable of trivialising important matters as she was of making a mountain out of a molehill.

'I have a spare mattress,' Daníel said. 'How long are you planning to stay?'

'Only for a few days, darling. A few days. I have a show every night this week, and it's too much of a hassle to drive to and from the countryside each time.'

'I thought you'd ride here,' he said, jokingly, then immediately regretted the choice of words. Lady Gúgúlú would be sure to put a spin on them. And she did.

'Riding me costs more than the fare from Selfoss to Hafnarfjörður.' She marched down the side of the house to the front door and vanished into Daníel's apartment.

'Actually, I meant on your horse,' he murmured, trailing after the drag queen, bearing her luggage.

Lady had installed herself in the kitchen, and when Daníel walked in was removing her false eyelashes with loud squeals. 'Oops, I went a bit overboard with the glue.' Then she took off her wig and plonked it in the middle of the kitchen table, where it sat like a splendid ornament at a grand seventeenth-century banquet.

Daníel joined her at the table and contemplated his friend. As she removed the layers of make-up with a series of single-use wet wipes, Lady slowly fell away, allowing her inner man, Róbert Þór, to emerge. 'Don't worry, they're biodegradable, made from corn and tapioca fibre. Environmentally friendly and moistened with aloe vera.'

'Actually, I was thinking how good it is to see you again,' said Daníel.

'Likewise, darling. You're looking well. Beavering in the garden, as ever, I see. Have you come across any elves lately?'

Daníel gave a rather awkward grin. Gúgúlú had nearly tricked him into believing there was some sort of enchanted patch at the bottom of the garden, protected by the hidden folk who lived in the rocks there. It was an example of how, if you repeat something to someone enough times, it can work its way into their head. He had learned about this on a course he'd attended on interrogation techniques, where they were warned against putting words into suspects' mouths.

Changing the subject, Daníel responded to Róbert's question with another, and instantly regretted it. 'How's the English boyfriend?'

Róbert's vehement response sounded more befitting of Lady. 'Not a topic for discussion. In fact, there's a ban on the subject until at least the autumn. Ask me about the horse instead.'

'How's the horse?'

'Wonderful, darling. Thank you for asking! Just imagine, I've sent it to some sort of pasture for horses, where it prances about and grazes on heather, free as a neutron to define its own space.'

16

Áróra was sitting at a table at the back of the restaurant, absorbed in the photographs of Ísafold on her phone. She scrolled through pictures of her and her sister when they were little, which her mum had scanned and sent to her, as well as photos she'd repeatedly transferred between phones, always intending to print out hard copies but never getting round to it. Photographs of Ísafold and Björn, and of the three of them together, when everything was hunky dory.

She had pointed at something on the menu the waiter had brought her, but had already forgotten what food she'd ordered. Her mind was in turmoil and right now she couldn't focus on anything except Ísafold. She felt a wave of pain go through her as she contemplated a photo of her and her sister laughing together on the sofa at the apartment in Engihjalli. This was how Ísafold had been. Cheerful and positive; fun-loving and always up for a laugh. She had never taken life seriously, the way Áróra did. She looked so relaxed and carefree in this picture, her face creased with laughter, and Áróra was sure Björn hadn't started hitting her then. The photo was probably taken the first time Áróra visited them. She'd enjoyed herself, and quite liked Björn. She'd found it a bit odd the way he kept calling Ísafold silly, but it sounded affectionate enough, and Ísafold seemed to think it was charming. Later, she told Áróra that Björn was always making out she was stupid. And later still Ísafold began to believe it herself.

'Can I get you anything else?' the waiter asked as he cleared away her plate, and it took Áróra a few seconds to remember she was sitting in a restaurant and had just wolfed down an entire meal almost without noticing.

'No, thank you,' she told the waiter. 'Just the bill, please.' Roused from her memories, Áróra felt the pain come flooding back, predictable as the tide, and she remembered the heart. Her sister's missing heart.

She drained her glass of water to wash away the lump rising in her throat, and felt the familiar heaviness on her chest that made it difficult to breathe. If only she had stood by Ísafold a bit longer. If only she had responded to her sister's cries for help that last time. Of course, Daníel was right when he said you couldn't help people who didn't want to be helped, and that Áróra couldn't take responsibility for her sister. But that's where Áróra's head and heart diverged. In her head she agreed with Daníel; in her heart she was convulsed with guilt whenever she recalled her last phone conversation with her sister.

'Perhaps you'd like to see the dessert menu?' asked the waiter, who was once more standing next to her table. Áróra realised the bill had been sitting there on the little dish for a while.

'Sorry, no thank you.' She placed her debit card on top of the bill and the waiter went to fetch the card machine.

She managed to pay and leave the restaurant without plunging back into mournful thoughts about Ísafold, but once in her car she opened the photo gallery in her phone again and continued to flick through the images. Ísafold dressed up for a dance. Her and Ísafold in identical tracksuits, she herself big and strong, Ísafold so small and delicate in comparison. Ísafold and Björn smiling, each with a cocktail in their hand. Ísafold with a black eye. Áróra gave a start. This was one of the photos she'd taken after Björn had beaten Ísafold up particularly badly, and Áróra had come over to Iceland to help her. Or to try to help her. For it hadn't been possible to help Ísafold, in fact. No matter how badly Björn treated her and no matter how hard Áróra tried to save her, Ísafold always went back to him.

17

'I just don't understand what you're thinking with this,' Ísafold said, and shook her head forlornly. Björn had finally told her what it was he wanted. He wanted her to give up her job at the clothing store in the shopping mall and look for work at a residential home.

'You're not the sharpest knife in the drawer, though, are you?' he said with a smirk, and she laughed. She didn't feel like laughing, but this had become the pattern with them. Whenever Björn implied she wasn't too bright, Ísafold would laugh as if he was teasing her. And at the beginning of their relationship, she really did believe he was joking when he said things like that. But then it dawned on her that it wasn't a joke; he actually thought she was a bit simple. And in the end, she began to believe he was probably right. Still, she went on laughing, as if it were funny.

'Why would I give up a steady, well-paid job for a minimum-wage, zero-hours contract?' She was relieved, of course, that Björn had finally told her what had been on his mind these last few days, but it still came as a shock. She had imagined numerous scenarios, but this wasn't one of them.

'Think about the interactions you have with people at Kringlan; they're so superficial,' he said. 'You'd be much happier working as a carer. You've always talked about how you like people.'

Björn was right, in a way; she had sometimes said she wished she could chat more with the customers who visited the store. At the same time, she realised that Björn's sudden concern about her social relationships wasn't the whole story. She felt utterly confused.

'But I'll probably earn thirty thousand krónur a month less at a residential home than in my current job,' she protested feebly, knowing there was no use her arguing. When Björn had the bit *between his teeth about something, it was hopeless to try to make him change his mind.*

His face clouded over and she wished she hadn't insisted so much. 'What makes you think I care about your shitty thirty thousand krónur, Ísafold, huh? In the big scheme of things? Do you think it makes any fucking difference?'

She shook her head mutely. There was something he wasn't telling her.

'No, probably not,' she murmured softly, aware of her pulse throbbing louder and louder in her head until it became like a metronome ticking in her ears. She felt the apartment contract around her, squeezing her, threatening to become so tight she couldn't move or breathe.

'Just trust me,' he said. 'First and foremost I'm thinking of your well-being. You know everything I do is for you.'

Björn always said this. That everything he did was for her. But when she thought about it, he didn't actually do very much. A half-day shift, and the rest of the time he spent chatting to his mates on the phone or in front of the computer. She did most of the housework and shopping, and if anything in the apartment needed fixing, she saw to that too.

Björn went into the bathroom and she heard him turn on the shower. Seized by a sudden impulse, she grabbed the spare set of house keys, rushed out into the corridor and down the stairs, where she knocked on Grímur's door.

'If you think it sounds like he's killing me, call the police and give them the keys, so they can come in and rescue me,' she rattled out when he opened the door. 'I don't have time to chat right now,' she said then, hastening away. As she turned the corner of the staircase, she glimpsed Grímur watching her with that expression she used to think was coldness, but now realised was an effect of his baldness. On the contrary, Grímur was a kind man who had been a good friend to her, even if he did insist on singing the same old song as

her sister Áróra. About how she should leave Björn. She knew they meant well. But neither of them understood that it was easier said than done.

Back upstairs, she was relieved to hear the shower still running in the bathroom.

TUESDAY

18

Áróra nuzzled up against Daníel's warm back and breathed in his scent. He had crawled into bed sometime before midnight and whispered to her how glad he was that she'd come round. She had murmured something, pretending to be asleep, as she was still not ready to talk to him, even though her longing to have him close had compelled her to sleep over at his place instead of going home alone, which had been her original plan.

Now, however, she could no longer avoid facing him. She got out of bed, went into the bathroom and jumped in the shower. As the hot water flowed over her face, she searched for the right words to express what was on her mind. A good night's sleep had made her feel better and provided a much-needed break from her endless thoughts of Ísafold.

Daníel had her coffee ready when she came into the kitchen in her underwear, her wet hair wrapped in a towel. She had some vague notion of the lecture she was going to give him about how relationships couldn't thrive when people kept secrets, but when he gazed at her with those gentle eyes of his and said softly, 'I'm sorry', suddenly it felt redundant. She didn't need to explain anything to him. She could see he knew exactly how she felt. That was what made Daníel so special. His uncanny ability to open his heart to her completely, and to understand her emotions. She walked over to him and placed her arms about him. He held her close and whispered in her ear once more: 'I'm sorry.'

Then they sat down at the table, each with their cup of coffee in front of them.

'Do they have any theories?' she asked. As she'd expected, Daníel shook his head.

'I don't think so.'

'How about you?' she went on.

Daniel gave a faint smile. 'None at all,' he said. 'We've not seen anything like this before here in Iceland, apart from a few isolated instances when a murder was carried out by someone having a psychotic episode. Then a lot of weird stuff can happen, but this doesn't fit that pattern. It's too organised, and ... How shall I put it? Neat. Bodies in suitcases left in a remote location. None of the chaos you find with a psychotic killer.'

'Do you promise to keep me in the loop from now on?' She stared straight at Daníel to drive her point home, and he smiled again.

'I'll do my best, my love,' he replied. 'Gutti seems determined to prevent any leaks between teams, though I confess to having listened in more than I normally would on an investigation I'm not involved in. What I will do is ask Gutti to make a point of updating you on any developments. You should also ask your mother to do the same. As Ísafold's closest relative, the police liaise with her about the case.'

Áróra nodded. She wasn't looking forward to talking to her mother. Perhaps she should wait another day or two. Allow her emotions time to settle, her head to clear a little more. She was liable to fly off the handle otherwise, say things she regretted. She drained her cup and passed it to Daníel, indicating she wanted another coffee. He rose and went over to fiddle with the coffee machine.

'I'm working on a new case,' he said. 'Something to do with money-laundering.'

'Sounds good,' Áróra said.

He laughed. 'Maybe for you. Financial crime doesn't usually float my boat. Although my role on this one is to check if there's anything suspicious about...'

His last words were drowned out by the noise of the milk frother. The coffee machine was a recent gift from Áróra, and she and Daníel had quickly established a kind of ritual around it. Two lattes each in the mornings and an espresso after dinner. And Daníel always prepared them. It seemed to have brought out the latent barista in him, and he wore a proud expression whenever he brought over a cup of coffee he'd conjured from his machine.

'Do you know anything about Kaffikó?' he asked, passing her a latte. The frothed milk stood proud of the rim and Áróra leaned forward to sip from the cup.

'Are you planning to ask them for a job?' she said teasingly.

'You never know,' he laughed. 'I'll need to practise my frothing technique first.'

'And your cinnamon sprinkling. You have to learn to make a heart or a leaf pattern, or something, in order to apply.' He grinned, then his grin turned into a sort of grimace. 'Why do you ask?' Áróra went on, setting down her cup.

'Oh, just that I heard something about it being an unusually profitable company. It's probably nothing. Just something I picked up in passing.'

19

Felix had felt a knot of anxiety in his stomach since one of the boys called to say Sturla wanted to talk to him right away. He had leapt to his feet, pulled on some clothes, managed to tamp down his hair with some water, then sprayed himself liberally with aftershave, before rushing out. He drove at speed up to Grafarholt, even though the last thing he wanted was to arrive – because he was scared shitless. What did Sturla want with him this early in the morning? It was probably about yesterday's collection not being good enough. He'd given a couple of the small-time dealers another week to pay what they owed in full; he'd been doing that quite a lot lately, even though he knew it would piss Sturla off.

He came to a halt outside the row of terraced houses and took a deep breath. The morning sun was warm and the sound of birdsong seemed to reach him from every direction. He rang the bell and closed his eyes, silently praying Sturla wasn't planning to make him undergo one of his notorious tests, some ordeal through which he was to prove himself a loyal and trustworthy servant.

He was astonished when Sturla himself opened the door. Usually, it was one of his boys, who acted like bodyguards, frisking all newcomers, and wore permanently sullen expressions. However, this time Sturla had come to the door in person, and stranger still, he was smiling.

'Good morning, my friend!' he said cheerily, clapping Felix on the shoulder. 'Today I'm sending you on a special errand.'

Felix didn't dare permit himself to be curious, and waited with bated breath to hear what it was he had to do. Something difficult and dangerous and dreadful, no doubt. Sturla had ordered one of his boys to steal a car and ram a storefront. The lad in question had done the deed and managed to flee on foot before the police showed up, leading Sturla to deem him one hundred percent trustworthy. Another boy was sent to burgle the home of a well-known mixed-martial-arts fighter and make off with a trophy Sturla coveted, and which now sat on a shelf in his living room, as if Sturla had won it himself.

On this occasion, however, Sturla seemed in a good mood and radiated friendliness. 'I'm entrusting you to drive to Seyðisfjörður to fetch a package that's due to arrive with the ferry,' he said, placing his hand on Felix's shoulder again and squeezing it gently, even as his face grew solemn. 'It's not without risk, and you'll need to have your wits about you, but I have every confidence in you.'

Felix gave Sturla's words time to sink in, and weighed them up in his mind. Sturla wasn't setting a trap for him. He was entrusting him with one of the most important jobs in the business.

'Thanks, Sturla,' he said, doing his best to conceal his emotion. 'I won't let you down.'

'Excellent!' Sturla said, removing his hand from Felix's shoulder and taking a set of keys from the shelf in the hallway. He handed them to Felix. 'You'll take Bangsi's car. It's damn fast, and a cool ride. It's outside waiting for you. Just make sure you don't break the speed limit.'

Felix felt a frisson of joy as he took the keys. Bangsi's car was a brand-new Audi SUV and he looked forward to testing its power on the drive to Seyðisfjörður.

'We have a tracker on the car, so we'll be monitoring you. And remember, no phone calls.'

'Of course not,' Felix said. He wasn't stupid, but then maybe a lot of Sturla's boys were.

He waved to Sturla as he walked towards the car, then slipped into the soft leather seat that cooed gently as it moulded itself to his body. Today would be anything but dull. He knew he risked several years in prison if he was caught with the package, but it also meant a two-day road trip, playing his music at full volume, eating fast food at every stop. In addition, he wouldn't have to put the squeeze on a single person. He sped off down the street, beaming with contentment. All he had to do today was drive.

Turning east onto Suðurlandsvegur, a sudden feeling of unease crept over him. Had Sturla sent him on this errand because he was unhappy with how lenient he was with his debtors? Was it actually some kind of punishment or test? He pondered this for a while, but when he reached Kambarnir and saw the landscape of South Iceland spread out before him, he made a firm decision to stop worrying. He would successfully carry out the task and enjoy himself in the process.

The engine purred sweetly beneath him, carrying him at a terrifying speed towards the unknown.

20

What was this thing with Canada? Helena thought. Áróra's remark had been troubling her since they bumped into one another outside the apartment block yesterday. She'd since discovered that although Olga wasn't especially active on social media, she posted on Facebook whenever she had some big event on the horizon: Christmas, Easter, finishing an Icelandic wool sweater she was knitting, new tiles for her balcony, yet another visit to Canada. Scrolling quickly back through two years of Olga's posts, Helena had come across a photograph of her with a young man. He'd apparently tagged Olga in the photo, which explained why it was on her timeline. The man looked Arabic but had quite fair skin. His name was Snæþór Ómar. Helena tapped on his profile, but it was locked so she was unable to see any other posts. She considered sending him a friend request but decided to wait with that. In the post in which he'd tagged Olga, he appeared to give thanks for his good fortune, according to auto-translate, anyway, as the message was in Arabic: 'Finally, life is good again, praise be to Allah and all those who follow his path.' As well as Olga, he had tagged a man named Ásgrímur. Helena gave a start. The profile picture was old, and in it the man still had hair and eyebrows, but there was no mistaking. It was Grímur from the block on Engihjalli.

Helena printed out the post and laid it on the desk before her. Why would this young man in Canada be thanking Grímur? Was he perhaps a relative of Olga's who had visited her in Iceland and become acquainted with Grímur? This was as far as she'd got with her train of thought when Vala strode in and plonked a paper cup down in front of her.

'Here you are, café latte,' she said.

'I already have a coffee,' Helena said, pointing to the cup of watery police-station brew.

'I'll bet you anything this tastes better,' Vala chortled. 'Especially with a doughnut.' She deposited a paper bag on the desk, too, before taking her parka off and draping it over her chair.

Helena succumbed to temptation, tore open the bag, grabbed a *kleinur*, and bit into the traditional Icelandic fried doughnut. 'These *kleinur* from Kaffikó are delicious,' she said with her mouth half full, and Vala smiled contentedly.

'That was brilliant what you said yesterday, about homophobia and racism, even if you did lie about it being my main thesis. The way that immigration woman freaked, it was crazy.'

Helena grinned. She only wished Sirra had been as appreciative of her heroism. Their evening had been spent consoling Bisi, assuring her she wasn't about to be detained and deported to Nigeria.

'I'm pretty sure it was the old couple next door who reported us. They've seemed very preoccupied about how dark-skinned Bisi is. They've also tried to warn me that she and Sirra are in an unnatural relationship.'

Vala burst into laughter then looked searchingly at Helena. 'Are you a throuple?'

Helena choked on her coffee. 'What?'

'You know, three in a couple – polyamory? I just sensed something strange in the air yesterday.'

'I see. No, no, we're not a throuple. I'm just renting Sirra and Bisi's front room while I have some work done on my apartment. They're good friends of mine, and we get along really well.'

'It's all so exotic, somehow,' Vala said, munching on a doughnut. 'I've always dreamed of living with a group of lesbian friends in a commune, hanging out together the whole time and being involved in one another's lives, like in *The L Word*.'

'Hm. Are you saying you're one of us?' Helena asked.

Vala gave a big grin. 'Of course! Hadn't you figured that out yet?'

'Er, no. I hadn't realised. You're such a – how shall I put it? – cis-femme type.'

'Thank you,' Vala said cheerfully, fluttering her long eyelashes so that Helena almost choked on her coffee.

'I didn't particularly mean that as a compliment. It was more an ... observation.'

Vala smiled again, and Helena cleared her throat as she pointed at the print-out of Snæþór Ómar Facebook post on her desk.

'Look at this,' she said. 'This is Olga, who we were going to try to get hold of yesterday. And this is the young man she's apparently visiting in Canada, who also tagged our friend Grímur in his message of thanks.'

Vala considered the photograph. 'Interesting,' she said, and Helena nodded, giving way to temptation and reaching for a second *kleinur*.

21

After Áróra left, Daníel picked up his laptop and installed it on the kitchen table. He was sipping his second coffee and reading an article that mentioned Kaffikó, when he heard the familiar creak of the porch door opening.

'Morning, darling!' Lady Gúgúlú said, as she strode in wearing a dressing gown with a towel twisted into a turban on her head. She made a beeline for the fridge and began rummaging around for something for breakfast.

'There's bread in the freezer you can toast,' Daníel said, and Lady followed his advice, putting two slices into the toaster.

'And what plans do you have on this glorious day, Daníelito?'

'Oh, same old, same old. Chasing villains. Actually, I've been relegated to investigating a financial-crimes case, and financial crime bores me silly.'

'Then it should be easy for you to ask Áróra to help you out.' Lady paused. 'By the way, is she still on the map?'

Daníel grinned. 'Yes. She's still on the map, though I always feel it's a bit touch and go.'

'Nothing's changed, then, I see.' Lady proceeded to slather what looked to Daníel like a quarter of a tub of butter on her toast, before casting a meaningful glance at the coffee machine.

'I'll do it,' Daníel said, rising to his feet.

'Triple caramel macchiato, darling.'

Daníel had no idea how to make a macchiato, then remembered vaguely that it was an espresso with a dash of milk.

'I don't have any caramel, but you can have sugar instead,' he said. 'How are things at the country estate?'

Lady sat down, placing her toast directly on the kitchen table.

'That's a very good question,' she said, wrinkling her brow.

'The house is relatively stable, but the land around it is like a quantum particle, in a state of perpetual flux. It's as if the earth itself dances to an unpredictable rhythm, breaking apart and re-assembling itself in a way that's neither foreseen nor immediately comprehensible.'

Daníel raised his eyebrows quizzically. 'Do you mean the land there is geothermal or are you describing the changing seasons, or ... what are you saying?'

Lady took a bite of her toast. 'No, it's not geothermal,' she said. 'Although the state or condition of a thing is of course connected with perspective, right? Everything seeks equilibrium, yet perspective always has to take into account whether you're positively or negatively charged.'

'I see,' Daníel replied. He was enjoying himself. Although he had next to no understanding of quantum physics, and couldn't be sure whether what Lady was bombarding him with was indeed quantum physics or complete gobbledygook. He had missed these moments. It was always fun to begin his day pondering one of Gúgúlú's riddles.

As he left the kitchen, he clapped her on the shoulder.

'I've missed you, Gúgú,' he said.

22

Áróra was already immersed in the affairs of Kaffikó when Daníel called to ask if she'd take a quick look at the management side of their business. She'd gone straight to her computer when she got home, certain that Daníel wouldn't have asked her about Kaffikó that morning unless it was connected with the investigation he said he was working on. She felt excited about it. Moreover, it was a great relief to have something else to think about, other than Ísafold and the missing heart. Now, though, she refrained from telling Daníel she'd already looked at the company's reports going back three years, scrutinised several of their annual financial statements from the same period, and compared the data with that of two other coffeehouse chains. Before saying anything to him, she wanted to look into them more in-depth, as there was indeed something odd about Kaffikó's accounts.

Kaffikó was a successful company. Áróra had trawled the online media for stories about the company and found everywhere praise. There were two other coffeehouse chains in Iceland that had been operating longer than Kaffikó and had built their businesses on the back of the global resurgence of coffee as a popular drink. This was when the big global chains began selling coffee in places with fashionable interiors, drawing in a younger clientele. Kaffikó was a relative newcomer: the company had been operating for six years and placed a special emphasis on attracting tourists by offering the fried doughnuts, or *kleinur*, traditionally served with coffee in Iceland. However, to the unexpected delight of the owners, it turned out Icelanders also enjoyed a *kleinur* with their coffee, which – if the posts on Kaffikó's website were anything to go by – took them back to the small, dense, home-baked fried doughnuts of their youth.

Examining the annual financial statements of the three companies, Áróra found it curious that despite having fewer coffeehouses, Kaffikó seemed considerably more profitable than its two competitors. How had Kaffikó managed to earn nearly double the profits of the other two? It wasn't as if Kaffikó's coffeehouses were in prime locations – on the contrary. Nor could the fact that they attracted more tourists explain the increased revenue, since the other two chains had branches much closer to the city's main tourist attractions, whereas the majority of those owned by Kaffikó were on the outskirts of the most popular neighbourhoods, and therefore more difficult to reach on foot. Áróra frowned. Something here wasn't quite right.

There was a limit to the amount of information Áróra could glean from annual financial statements and company reports. She needed to dig deeper to get to the bottom of this discrepancy. And she could only do so by inspecting the company's accounts more closely. That meant going into work and convincing Agla of the need to take several random samples from the accounting records of the coffeehouse businesses. Although in her head Áróra thought of it as *going into work*, she wasn't in fact employed by the Directorate of Tax Investigations. They hired her occasionally, always on a short contract, and she sold them information, which she either acquired or obtained for herself from foreign data leaks. It was amazing how many Icelanders kept their money stashed away in tax havens.

She stood up from the table, shut her laptop and slipped it into her rucksack. Daníel needed her help, and given he'd called to ask her to look into Kaffikó, it had to be important. She'd head straight over to see Agla, to prepare the way for taking a proper look into the company. Maybe she'd stop off for a coffee at one of their coffeehouses, drink in the atmosphere of the place, so to speak. This had piqued her curiosity.

23

Daníel had managed to muster a shred of curiosity about Marteinn and Gyða, the main owners of Kaffikó. A search on the police database revealed the couple had reported three acts of vandalism to their property in the past five years. The first incident took place five years ago at one of their coffeehouses, and in the past year there had been two separate incidents. Someone keyed their car, scratching the bodywork all the way round, and a rock was thrown through a window at their house. It was somewhat unusual for people to be the victims of vandalism this many times; however, they did live in the city centre, where people going home drunk after a night out were apt to get up to all kinds of mischief. In any case, it gave him a pretext to speak directly to the couple.

As he parked outside the Kaffikó coffeehouse on Sæbraut, Daníel found himself taking a deep breath to try to work up some enthusiasm for the task ahead; he disliked this type of interview, which involved beating about the bush to conceal the real reason behind his investigation. Yet here he was with his phony smile, friendly gestures and a reason to speak to a man in whom Europol was interested.

Marteinn was sitting at a table at the back of the café and rose smiling to his feet when Daníel walked in. 'I've asked the kids to prepare a small selection of pastries for you,' he said. 'To give you an idea of our concept.'

Daníel would have liked to decline, but the hot dog he'd eaten for lunch hadn't exactly filled him up, and when a young man came scurrying over with a large plate that he set on the table in front of Daníel, he decided to kick off proceedings using the friendly-chat technique. He removed his jacket, slung it over the back of the chair and while Marteinn dashed back and forth to the counter, to ensure Daníel received a cup of their finest coffee, he began sampling the pastries. The freshly baked happy marriage cake was moist and delicious, the jam a tiny bit chewy, the way his grandma made it.

'This is excellent,' he said to Marteinn, who had come back carrying a huge mug containing what looked like a litre of coffee with some foamy latte art on top.

Marteinn beamed contentedly. 'Nothing beats good old traditional recipes,' he said, sitting down at the table again. He closed his laptop and looked amiably at Daníel as he munched noisily on a crêpe.

'Do you work here, on the premises?' Daníel asked between mouthfuls, and Marteinn nodded. He was the stereotypical young entrepreneur. A man who knew what he wanted from life, and pursued a winning idea with determination. Daníel could easily imagine a business magazine like *Viðskiptablaðið* doing a two-page spread on the couple.

'Here, there and everywhere,' Marteinn said. 'We prefer not to have a headquarters. Those of us who run the business bring our laptops to the various coffeehouses, where we can sit and work, and at the same time keep an eye on things. That way we're close to both our staff and our customers, and it's easy for us to intervene if necessary.'

'And you can always get good coffee,' Daníel said, sipping from the enormous mug, and Marteinn chuckled. Daníel bit into a freshly fried *kleinur*, took another sip of coffee and nodded appreciatively at Marteinn, who watched him excitedly.

'Good, aren't they?'

'Amazing,' said Daníel. 'Just like the ones my grandma makes.'

'Yes, Gyða and I decided to do exactly that – use our mothers' and grandmothers' recipes, and it seems to have awakened a lot of fond memories in people.' Daníel nodded as he munched, then Marteinn raised his eyebrows inquiringly and gave a little cough.

'So, what can I do to assist the police?' he asked.

Daníel washed down the last morsel of *kleinur* with a mouthful of coffee then dabbed his lips.

'I'm carrying out a sort of housekeeping exercise. Looking back at petty crimes that have been forgotten in the system, to see whether the cases were closed without being logged, or whether in fact they remain unsolved.' This was complete nonsense but might ring true to someone who knew nothing about police working methods. Daníel wasn't sure whether Marteinn bought his explanation, but judging from his expression he looked utterly confused.

'I believe you and your wife reported several acts of vandalism. Yourself on two separate occasions, and your wife Gyða once.' Daníel didn't need to elaborate, because Marteinn pulled a face.

'Ah,' he said. 'That old story. Frankly, it was no big deal. Someone broke into our first coffeehouse and smashed the place up. On another occasion our car was keyed, and not long after someone put a rock through a window at our house on Lindargata. Nothing came of the investigation. I expect it was some young hoodlums amusing themselves at our expense.' Daníel contemplated Marteinn's face as he trotted this out. He didn't seem ruffled, but Daníel sensed a certain unease.

'So, the case – or cases – aren't in fact closed?' Daníel said, picking up his notebook and pretending to jot something down.

'No, but the police needn't waste any more time on this. The insurance company covered the damage to the coffeehouse and the car, and replacing one windowpane wasn't a big outlay.'

'Still, it must make you uncomfortable not knowing who was behind this?'

Marteinn shrugged. 'No, no,' he said. 'We're not the sort of people who dwell on the past. It happened a long time ago.'

'The damage to your house only occurred last year,' Daníel said, slightly surprised that the man didn't seem to want to know who might have it in for them.

'Oh, really? It feels longer ago than that. In any case, you can cross it off your list. It's not something we want to pursue.'

'That's what law enforcement is for,' Daníel said, smiling. 'So we do need to take another look at this. I'd like to speak with your wife, if possible, to see whether she remembers something that wasn't in the original report. Will she be at home now?'

Now Marteinn's feathers seemed ruffled, and Daníel could almost see how his inner peace had been disrupted. It was always useful to get past the defences most people carefully erected around themselves and catch a glimpse of what was happening within. And inside, Marteinn was seething.

'Yes, she should be at home. But look here, are you seriously going to waste time on this kind of trivia? Don't the police have better things to do?' he snapped, with a trace of righteous indignation. Daníel felt his curiosity quicken. What on earth was it about this matter that upset the man so much?

'It's standard police procedure to revisit unsolved cases. Don't worry, we won't need to bother you. And I won't keep your wife for very long. I'd just like to hear her side of the story,' he said, broadening his phony smile.

Marteinn took a couple of deep breaths, as if to steady himself. Then he exhaled slowly, blowing his cheeks out like a trumpet player.

'We're extremely busy people; we run a substantial business,' he muttered, the same indignant expression on his face.

'I'll be sure to take that into account,' Daníel said, closing his notebook and slipping it in his breast pocket.

He rose and made his way towards the door, stopping off at the counter to pay for his refreshments.

24

Agla, team manager at the Directorate of Tax Investigations, looked sceptical when Áróra proposed taking random samples from three coffeehouse businesses. Clearly, she would need some convincing. Although more adventurous than some of her fellow civil servants, Agla wouldn't move on a case unless she saw a clear advantage in it. She and Áróra enjoyed a good working relationship. This mostly revolved around Áróra handling the investigative tasks public officials weren't at liberty to look into, and on a few occasions Áróra had sold her information regarding investments that Icelandic citizens held in offshore companies and had 'forgotten' to declare.

'It's pointless simply playing endless hide-and-seek with the oil and fishing industries,' Áróra said, perching on the edge of Agla's desk. 'There's a lot of money-laundering in the restaurant sector, and I sense something fishy about Kaffikó. Their turnover is way higher than that of their competitors.'

'Isn't that because they attract more tourists?' Agla asked. 'It's easy to overcharge foreigners who have zero price-consciousness and no clue about what things cost here in Iceland.'

Áróra had anticipated this response. 'That's exactly what they claim, that they mainly cater to tourists. But I have the feeling this isn't entirely true.' She pulled a map of Reykjavík from her back pocket, and spread it out on the desk in front of Agla. On it she had marked the locations of Kaffikó's coffeehouses with a red dot, and those of their competitors with a green dot. 'Look at this,' she said, picking up Agla's pen and marking crosses at various other locations. 'Here's the Sun Voyager sculpture, here's Hallgrímskirkja church, here's Tjörnin Pond, and here's the National Museum. Here, here and here are the most popular swimming pools.' She traced a few more lines on the map. 'This is the main shopping street, Laugavegur, this is Skólavörðustígur and this is Grandi. And here are Þingholt, Grjótaþorp, and the old quarter, Austurbær.'

'Hm.' Agla contemplated the map. 'I see what you mean,' she murmured. The crosses and lines were all close to the coffeehouses marked with green dots but not to those of Kaffikó marked with red dots.

'How can they possibly attract more tourists than their competitors when all their coffeehouses are further away from the main tourist attractions?'

Agla leaned back in her chair and gazed searchingly at Áróra. 'And you want me to supply you with sample accounting data from all three companies and then you'll sell me what you find?'

'Yes,' replied Áróra. 'That way, if I do find something, we both benefit.'

'Hm.' Agla continued to contemplate Áróra, as if she were trying to read her thoughts. 'How did this come up? Why have you been looking at Kaffikó's annual financial reports?'

'It could be connected to my boyfriend,' Áróra replied, putting on a mysterious face.

Agla sat up in her chair. 'Really?'

'Yes,' Áróra said. 'All I can tell you is that Kaffikó could be part of an ongoing investigation. And if some scandal were to break, it might look good for the Directorate of Tax Investigations to be able to say you were already investigating the company. It would show you have your finger on the pulse.'

'That I can use,' Agla said rising from her chair. 'Wait here a moment.'

Áróra watched her pass through the door and head down the corridor towards the office of the head of the Directorate of Tax Investigations himself, Agla's boss. Her pulse was racing a little with the excitement. Hopefully she hadn't gone too far by mentioning Daniel's name. And hopefully it would pay off.

25

Daníel glanced about the living room. Every object was in its right place. Even the grey woollen rug, apparently casually tossed onto the white sofa, was in fact carefully positioned. The colours were soft and muted, the furniture white or pine finish, and a row of scented candles in pastel tones that matched the cushions stood next to some magazines on a large tray on the coffee table. This home resembled a picture in a magazine about interiors, yet Daníel felt uneasy the minute he walked in there. He sensed a tension in the air, and it was clearly coming from Marteinn.

'Hello, again,' Marteinn said when Gyða ushered Daníel into the room.

'Oh, back home already,' Daníel said with a smile. 'That was quick.' He himself had driven straight from the coffeehouse to the couple's house on Lindargata, so Marteinn had clearly been in a hurry. Daníel was growing increasingly curious. Did Marteinn not want Gyða to talk to the police on her own?

'Let's begin at the beginning,' Daníel said, directing his words to Gyða. 'As I mentioned to your husband earlier, I'm looking into unsolved minor crimes. It seems that in the past five years you've reported three acts of vandalism, two of which took place in the last twelve months.'

Gyða glanced sideways at Marteinn before replying. 'It was probably some local kids,' she said, and Daníel detected a slight tremor in her voice. 'A few scratches on the car and a smashed window. The sort of thing that happens when kids muck around.' Gyða's eyes slid over to her husband once more.

Marteinn gave a little cough and looked pointedly at Daníel, before adding: 'Like I already told you.'

'May I ask which window they smashed?'

'That one,' Gyða replied, pointing to one of four south-facing windows on the opposite wall.

Daníel nodded, as if this were a significant piece of information, and walked over to the window in question. Like the others, it looked out onto a back garden, as well as part of the garden next door.

'So, whoever smashed your window did so either from your garden or that of your neighbour?' Daníel said. 'Have you been involved in any neighbourly disputes?'

'No,' Gyða said, forcing a smile. 'Nothing of that sort.'

Daníel returned her smile, and she visibly relaxed. Still, both Gyða and her husband were unusually tense. Of course a lot of people felt intimidated when talking to the police, or other agents of authority, but this was more than that.

'The incident took place in June, and you were at home at the time. Did you see anyone?'

'No.'

'Really?' Daníel looked straight at Marteinn, who shook his head.

'No.'

'And you didn't go outside to take a look around after the rock came through your window?'

'No,' Gyða said, flustered. 'We were too scared.'

'Well, scared is perhaps too strong a word,' Marteinn murmured, 'but it was certainly unnerving. We didn't want to risk having a rock aimed at our head.'

'Did you, or do you, have any enemies?' Daníel asked, and Gyða hesitated, glanced at her husband, who once again answered for them both:

'No, but when you're in business, as we are, there will always be people you have dealings with who aren't a hundred percent satisfied.'

This sounded promising. 'I see.' Daníel jotted it down in his notebook, and when he looked up, he saw the couple exchange nervous glances once more. 'Is something the matter?' he asked, and they seemed to recoil as one.

'No, nothing,' Marteinn said, and Gyða laughed apologetically. For a moment, an awkward silence descended, and then a big white Labrador came lumbering into the room and jumped up to greet Daníel. He crouched down on one knee, scratched the dog's head and received a lick on the chin.

'Who's this?' he asked, smiling.

The dog's timely entrance had dissipated the tension in the room.

'Pjakkur.' Gyða beamed, apparently pleased that Daníel was a dog-lover.

Marteinn grabbed the dog by the collar and pulled it away from Daníel. 'He's still a puppy, and he's deaf as a post. If he's asleep he won't hear guests arrive, but as soon as he realises people are here, he launches a surprise attack.'

'He's gorgeous,' Daníel said, smiling at the couple. 'And obviously very friendly.' They beamed back at him like proud parents.

Daníel buttoned up his jacket and put his notebook in his pocket. 'Thank you for the information,' he said. 'I'll be in touch if I have any further questions.'

The dog followed Daníel out to the hallway, as though eager to leave with him, and he had to crack open the front door in order to slip out.

26

Björn's anger filled the living room. His voice ricocheted off the walls as he accused Ísafold of betrayal, of making empty promises, called her deceitful and a waste of space. She hadn't given him an exact date when she would hand in her notice at the store. She apologised profusely.

'I keep meaning to, I just haven't got round to it yet,' she said. 'We've been so busy I haven't had a free moment to speak to my boss.'

'You can write him an email. Or a letter and leave it on his desk,' Björn said.

'Somehow it feels so impersonal, so cold, handing in my notice in that way after how kind he's been to me.'

'Is there something between you two?' Björn said, and Ísafold flinched. Björn was capable of working himself up into a fit of jealous rage over nothing. All it took was for a waiter to smile at her, or some strange man in the street to give her what Björn thought was a lingering look.

'Don't be silly, Björn. You know perfectly well that he's gay,' she said, laughing feebly. 'I just want to keep things friendly.'

'And is being friendly to your employer more important than keeping your promises to me?'

'Of course not!' Björn looked taken aback. Maybe she'd been too emphatic and her tone sounded accusatory. She quickly added in a softer voice: 'I've told you I'll hand in my notice, and I will, at the first chance I get.'

'Hm,' Björn contemplated her, and for an instant she was afraid he might lose his temper, jump at her and start hitting her, but instead he seemed to retreat into his own thoughts. He nodded a few times, grunted, then turned on his heel and left the room.

He went into the bathroom and shortly afterwards she heard him flush the toilet, then she heard the tap run for quite a while and assumed he was brushing his teeth. A little later the bathroom door opened and he came into the living room to say goodnight.

'I think I'll stay up and watch an episode of something,' Ísafold said, and he nodded, disappearing down the hallway to the bedroom.

She turned on the TV, stretched out on the sofa, and pulled a blanket over her. It wasn't yet ten o'clock – unusually early for Björn to go to bed. No doubt he was annoyed with her, but she felt relieved. He hadn't reacted too badly when she answered him back. Far better, in fact, than she would have expected. She even felt a twinge of pride.

27

Áróra had nothing to investigate while she waited for Agla to provide her with random samples from the coffeehouses' accounting records, and she could feel the empty spaces in her head slowly fill with sorrow. This was accompanied by resentment, though she didn't know who or what to direct it at, so it gradually merged with her sense of powerlessness – which had always been the worst feeling Áróra knew. Endless questions swirled about in her head, and as she marched round the cut-price supermarket, Krónan, filling her basket with this and that, she realised that the more attention she gave to this feeling of powerlessness and resentment, the more it overwhelmed her.

When she stopped next to the meat counter, the first thing that caught her eye were the black Styrofoam trays of lambs' hearts, and her automatic response was to drop her basket, turn on her heel and run out of the store before she threw up.

Five minutes later, she pulled up outside the U-shaped apartment block in Bakkahverfi. Daníel had advised her not to talk to anyone connected with the case, and she knew he'd said the same to them about her, but she couldn't help herself. Whenever she thought about the little girl, Ester Lóa, it always set off a tumult inside her. It wasn't so long ago that the little girl's parents had insisted their daughter claimed to be Ísafold reincarnated. And the child had said a few things that seemed to back up that claim. However, Ester Lóa had said nothing about the heart.

Áróra walked through the square garden to the block's main entrance. She pressed the doorbell and heard the voice of Ester Lóa's mother, Elísabet, then the lock made a buzzing sound and Áróra entered and mounted the stairs. Elísabet came to the door and invited Áróra inside, but instead of greeting her with her usual broad smile, she wore an anxious expression on her face.

'Lárus would prefer us not to have any contact,' she said.

Áróra nodded. 'Daníel says the same,' she replied, and embraced Elísabet, who hugged her tight.

'Good to see you, anyway,' Elísabet said, walking ahead of Áróra into the living room. 'Ester Lóa is at nursery school.'

Áróra sat down on the sofa. Everything in the room was just as before. The play corner on the rug over by the window, the toy boxes lined up along the wall.

'Has Ester Lóa said anything lately?' Áróra didn't need to explain that she was asking whether the child had mentioned something in connection with her sister's case.

Elísabet smiled apologetically. 'No,' she said. 'The episode seems to be fading. According to what we've read, this is what always happens. Children gradually grow out of it.'

'And memories become forgotten,' Áróra said, in a tone more solemn than she'd intended.

'Yes,' said Elísabet. Then she stood up, went out into the kitchen and returned carrying two small bottles of Coke. She handed one to Áróra and sat down again.

'I've just received new information about the case,' said Áróra. 'The police now seem convinced Björn didn't kill Ísafold. They believe a third party killed the two of them.'

Elísabet took a sip of Coke, swallowed and nodded a few times, as though considering how to respond.

'So, Ester Lóa was wrong about that?'

'It seems so,' Áróra said. 'She hasn't said anything else about Ísafold or Björn, or me?'

Elísabet shook her head. 'No, nothing.' Elísabet drained her Coke and set the empty bottle on the coffee table. 'I'm sorry, but I have to go. I have to pick up Ester Lóa early. She has an appointment with the cardiologist.'

Áróra felt goosebumps break out on her arms. 'A cardiologist? What for?'

'Didn't you know?' Elísabet asked. 'Ester Lóa was born with a heart defect. Nothing serious, but it needs to be monitored.'

28

Exhausted after the journey, Felix drove slowly down the hill to Seyðisfjörður. The stream of vehicles coming out of the fjord was continuous; they were mostly rental cars, a few people carriers, and then coaches. Lots of coaches. He wondered how many tourists had arrived on the ferry that day. Several hundred at least. And one of them had brought the package Felix was supposed to pick up.

He would never see the person, or know anything about them. Sturla made sure to keep the various links in his chain separate. Despite claiming to have complete trust in his men, he maintained that it was better for them if they knew as little as possible. Felix sometimes wondered whether there were some bigger guys behind Sturla. It was quite likely – not that it really mattered. He would never see them. It wasn't like with Björn, who behaved as if he were some big shot, but then the reality turned out to be quite different. Felix was only a teenager when he first ran errands for Björn, and back then he thought Björn was the coolest guy around. He wore the coolest clothes, always had a pretty girl on his arm, could afford anything he wanted. That is until Sturla came into their lives.

The view opened out onto the fjord, and the town curved like a horseshoe round the head of the fjord and the harbour, where the ferry lay like a great leviathan. Seen from above it appeared to tower over the town's buildings, as if a big toy boat had been plonked in the middle of a miniature play set. The bright colours of the houses glinted in the water, and Felix tried to recall which side of the fjord the guest house was on. He had a vague recollection it was near the harbour, but it was two years since Sturla sent him here on a similar trip with another boy, so he wasn't sure. A sudden pang of fear made his pulse quicken. What if he'd driven all this way and couldn't find the guest house? And he wasn't allowed to call to ask where it was. He felt the sweat break out on his back and he looked about desperately as he drove slowly through the town. He passed the ferry, and just as he came to the last row of houses, he spotted it. A grey-painted, corrugated-iron building with white window frames and an old ship's wheel hanging on the wall by the front door, on which the words *Bed and Breakfast* were written in English.

He parked on the gravelled area on one side of the house, and, as he climbed out of the car, breathed the cold, crisp air deep into his lungs. Everything was going to be fine. Of course, everything was going to be fine. No way would he mess this up.

A bell tinkled as he opened the door, and an old lady appeared in the hallway that had a small parlour on one side and a big kitchen on the other.

'Good evening,' the woman said. 'How may I help you?'

The place was cosy, the furnishings probably as old as the house, although the big green plants and pale-coloured walls gave it a modern feel.

Felix leaned towards her and said in a hushed voice, 'I have a room booked. Number seven, if I remember correctly.'

The woman smiled amiably. 'Yes. That's right. Room number seven.' She handed him a heavy bronze key and pointed to the stairs at the other end of the hallway. 'Breakfast tomorrow morning is between seven and nine.'

Felix thanked her, a wave of drowsiness washing over him. His bones seemed to grow heavier as he mounted the stairs. He'd reached his destination and couldn't wait to flop onto the bed and take a little nap before he went for a walk in the town to look for dinner and a toothbrush.

Felix closed the door behind him and locked out the world. He let himself fall onto the bed, which was soft and smelled of laundry soap. He longed to sink into it and drift off to sleep, but having lain there a while with his eyes closed, he realised the bag bothered him. The bag he'd come here to fetch, and which sat waiting for him on the small table over by the window, like any other innocent piece of tourist luggage.

He rose to his feet and lifted it slightly. It was made of leather, shaped like a sports bag, and was oddly heavy. Unzipping it cautiously, Felix peered inside and saw what looked like a piece of blue towelling. He fished it out. Underneath was a black plastic bag. He examined the bag until he found an opening and saw what was inside. Lots of small, vacuum-packed bundles – only they weren't the pills he was expecting. They were banknotes. He hurriedly zipped up the bag, as if he'd witnessed something he wasn't supposed to, then cautiously opened it again and inspected the vacuum-packed bundles. Most of them were euros, but some were pounds and three or four were Danish kronur. There wasn't a single packet of pills in the bag. It was stuffed with money.

29

Daníel stood in the middle of Lindargata and contemplated Gyða and Marteinn's detached house. After saying goodbye to the couple, he'd waited outside in his car and seen Marteinn leave a few minutes later. This presumably meant that Marteinn had come home specifically because he didn't want the police talking to Gyða on her own.

Daníel studied the houses to the left and right of the couple's large timber dwelling. On one side was an old cottage that had seen better days, on the other a large stone house on four floors, if you counted the semi-basement. Daníel trotted up the steps of the latter and inspected the doorbells. Only one had a name next to it. *Patrekur Benediktsson – Landlord.* On the others stood the numbers *101, 102, 104.* Daníel pressed the landlord's bell and before he knew it a thickset man came to the door. He wasn't exactly obese, but his rounded shoulders were broad and the fleshy folds on his neck gave him the appearance of a prize-fighter. He had a phone to his ear and raised his finger to indicate to Daníel to wait while he explained to someone in English how to take the airport coach to the city's bus terminal. The conversation confirmed what Daníel suspected, that this Patrekur, who referred to himself as 'landlord' on his doorbell, was just that. A landlord who rented out the other three apartments to tourists.

'So, you're in the hotel business,' Daníel said, after he'd introduced himself and Patrekur had invited him in.

'You could say that, yes. I own fourteen apartments here in the city centre,' he said. 'All of them taxed and licensed, of course,' he hastened to add.

'That's not what I came here to discuss,' Daníel said, slipping off his shoes. 'I'd like to talk to you about Gyða and Marteinn next door.'

Patrekur ushered Daníel through to the kitchen, which had a south-facing window, though, try as he might, Daníel couldn't see into Gyða and Marteinn's back garden from there because Patrekur's house extended too far back. Daníel sat down on a kitchen chair, which if it wasn't preloved sixties retro was an excellent reproduction.

'Do you know them at all?' he asked.

Patrekur shrugged. 'Yes, you could say that. I don't have much to do with them, but we occasionally bump into each other in the street, and then we might stop for a brief chat. I try to maintain good relations with my neighbours. It's essential when renting to tourists. You don't want people complaining.'

'So, they're good neighbours?'

'Yes, I'd say so. They seem nice enough.'

'Have you noticed a lot of visitors to their house, or anything – how shall I put this – unusual, anything that struck you as odd?'

Patrekur finally seemed to relax. He sat down on the chair opposite Daníel and gazed at him intently.

'No,' he replied. 'Why are you asking me about them?'

'They were victims of vandalism last year,' Daníel said.

'Yes, that was awful,' Patrekur said, shaking his head. 'Those poor people. And the police are only looking into this now?'

'No, not at all. We did our best when the case came up, but it was never solved. I'm going back over it to see whether anything new has emerged,' Daníel explained.

'I see. Of course. If there's anything I can do, just say the word. I'm at your service.' The man looked straight at Daníel and clenched his fist, as if he were offering to dig his car out of the snow or fell a large tree in his garden – something that required brute strength.

Daníel pulled out his notebook and pretended to flip through it. 'You didn't notice anything – when they had their car keyed, or when their window was smashed?'

'No, not then, no.' Patrekur wrinkled his nose. 'But I certainly did when their dog was killed.'

'Their dog?' Daníel gazed at the man in bewilderment.

'The whole neighbourhood must have heard Gyða's screams when she found the wretched animal in their back garden covered in blood. She woke up all my guests, who were terrified as it was the middle of the night.'

'Their dog was killed, you say? I had the impression I was patting it just now,' Daníel said, puzzled.

'No, that's their new dog,' Patrekur said. 'The old one had its throat cut last year. There must be something about it in your police records.'

30

Helena could tell from Vala's face that she was thinking the same thing they'd both thought yesterday: that Grímur's apartment wasn't as strange as his looks and character might lead you to expect. Aside from the rose-pattern sofa, the apartment was modern and there was a pleasant aroma from the scented candle burning on the window sill. Grímur himself, however, was stranger than ever, and it was clear these repeated visits from the police made him uneasy, to put it mildly.

After refusing a coffee, which Grímur apologised for neglecting to offer them the day before, but accepting a glass of water each, she and Vala sat down at the kitchen table, while Grímur perched on a chair opposite them, and seemed unable to get comfortable. Eventually, he sat bolt upright, hands on his knees, his body language contrived, like a model adopting a pose. Clearly it was difficult for him to maintain such a stiff posture.

'We need to ask you about this photograph,' Helena said. She placed on the table the photo she had printed from Olga's Facebook page, of Olga herself and the young man who called himself Snæþór Ómar.

'That's my neighbour, Olga,' Grímur said.

'And this man with her?'

Grímur narrowed his eyes and inspected the picture again. 'I've no idea. Possibly a relative of hers in Canada.'

'So, you've never met him?' Helena asked. 'His name is Snæþór Ómar.'

'I don't know any Snæþór,' Grímur said, and shook his head, while the rest of his body remained immobile, making the movement seem somewhat theatrical.

'What's strange is the caption,' Helena continued. 'It's in

Arabic, but when we translate it into a language we understand better, he seems to be thanking both you and Olga for something.'

'Really.'

Helena waited and when Grímur said nothing more, she proceeded.

'It doesn't ring any bells? Why this young man might be grateful to you?'

Grímur shook his head once more.

'It's strange, all these connections to Canada,' Helena mused, as she leaned back in her chair. She was thinking aloud rather than asking Grímur a direct question.

But he responded as if she were. 'What connections?' he said, a little too sharply.

'Only that Olga goes there so often. I saw on her Facebook page that she's been at least five times in four years. And then there's this young man in Canada thanking you both. Not forgetting, of course, Björn, who, after he disappeared, was last sighted at Toronto Airport. But then his body was discovered in a fissure on the Reykjanes peninsula.' Grímur didn't say anything but grunted a few times, so Helena went on. 'It's as if there's a channel running directly between this block here on Engihjalli and Canada.'

All of a sudden, Grímur sprang to his feet, slid his chair under the table and said in a loud voice: 'Well. I need to go. I have things to do.'

Then, after a brief pause, Helena said:

'Too bad. In that case I'll have to ask you to come down to the station tomorrow morning to finish our conversation. We need to go over this with you in more depth, so you can help us to identify the young man in the photograph. But we can do that in a formal interview setting, if you prefer.'

Grímur dragged his chair out again, sat down at the table and picked up the printed-out photograph. Vala cast an approving glance at Helena.

'On closer inspection,' Grímur said, making a show of bringing the photo right up to his face, 'this might be the lad Olga had staying with her for a while.'

'He stayed with Olga?'

'Yes, he was some sort of refugee who she took pity on. He was plain Ómar back then.'

'She took in a strange man off the street?' Helena realised how harsh her remark sounded, considering she and Sirra had done exactly that, and more.

'Yes,' Grímur said, a little hesitantly. 'Maybe she was acting from some motherly instinct, or making up for the son she lost.'

Helena took the case file from Vala and leafed through the transcript of Olga's interview.

'There's nothing in the report about a son,' Vala whispered. Helena took her word for it. She didn't doubt that Vala knew the case file off by heart.

'Olga's son died?'

'Yes, he died. He was one of the young lads Björn led astray.'

Helena's heart leapt.

'Wait a minute,' she said. 'Rewind a bit. Are you telling me Björn was a bad influence on Olga's young son?'

'It's no secret here in the neighbourhood that Björn had a group of young lads around him. He used them – how shall I put it? – to run errands for him.'

'Errands?' Vala cut in, pen poised. All of this was new to her, whereas Helena and the original investigative team had been well aware that Björn was involved in small-scale drug dealing. The information about Olga's son, however, was new.

'Yes, or whatever name he gave it: sales and distribution. I don't suppose it was anything more serious than doctor's dope and a bit of grass. He had his lads buy pills from the elderly and disabled. I know because I occasionally sold one of them some of my tranquillisers. I admit it was wrong. I shouldn't have done it. I feel bad about it, and I'd never do it again.'

Helena nodded vigorously to show that she fully believed all his excuses, and he could safely carry on talking.

'But why did those boys hang out with Björn?' she asked.

'Heaven knows. He did a bit of bodybuilding with them, played computer games, that kind of thing. He seemed to have them in his pocket, anyway. No doubt he gave them money or drugs in exchange for running his errands.'

'Did you know any of these boys?'

'Yes ... no – only Olga's son Jonni. He was among the first, but by the end Björn always had several lads from the neighbouring blocks – Guðmundur and Hallur and Felix, or whatever their names were. They became a bit lost when Björn disappeared. Guðmundur went the same way as Olga's Jonni – he got hooked on drugs and died.'

Silence reigned at the table for a few moments. Then Helena tapped the case file.

'Why didn't you tell us about the boys before?' she said, and she had scarcely finished her sentence when Grímur leapt to his feet, even more swiftly this time, and banged his fist hard on the table.

'I did!' he shouted. 'I told the police over and over again that Björn was using those young boys to sell drugs, and who listened to me? No doubt the same person who listened when I called repeatedly to tell you he was beating his wife up there. And look what came out of that?!'

Helena closed her eyes and sighed. 'I'm sorry Grímur, I didn't realise. All I have is the case file on Ísafold's and Björn's disappearance.'

She rose, extending her hand in a gesture of reconciliation, and when Grímur clasped hold of it she could feel he was trembling.

They took their leave, and on the way from the block to the car Helena realised her fixation with Canada hadn't diminished. If anything, it was stronger. Also of interest was the news that Björn had led Olga's son astray. It must mean that Olga detested Björn. Might she also have held a grudge against his girlfriend?

31

The music from the TV woke Ísafold with a start. It was the closing theme of some series she'd clearly slept right through. She rose to her feet, folded up the rug, placed it neatly on the sofa then turned off the lamp and the TV. She felt her way to the bathroom in the dark, only switching the light on after she'd closed the door so as not to disturb Björn. He found lights in the evening bothersome when he was trying to sleep. She used the loo, brushed her teeth, took her contraceptive pill then washed her face with hot water and a flannel mitten. She took out her various creams, and began with the eye cream Áróra had bought for her at the duty-free store. She rubbed it on the dark puffy shadows around her eyes that never seemed to go away, no matter how well she slept. Lastly, she applied her night cream and, switching off the light, tiptoed out of the bathroom into the bedroom.

Björn was asleep, and she gave a sigh of relief as she climbed into bed. His body was warm and soft beneath the duvet, and despite everything that had happened those past few weeks, despite being so often afraid of him, she always felt a reassuring sense of security whenever they lay in bed together. He stretched his arm out, placing it round her the way he always did, and she snuggled her backside into his lap, then bunched her pillow up under her head.

She had scarcely closed her eyes when her cheek began to itch. She pulled her hand from under Björn's arm to scratch it and gave a start. It felt as if her fingers were hot and had burned her skin. The itching swiftly spread to her entire face, and each time she scratched, she felt the same burning sensation on her skin.

She leapt out of bed, ran into the bathroom and turned on the tap. After soaking a towel in cold water she placed it over her face, but it only eased the burning for a few seconds. She washed her face carefully with soap and water, gently dabbing the flannel mitten on her cheeks and nose, her forehead and neck, but the burning only grew worse. She tried filling the basin with ice-cold water, leaning over it and splashing her face. She scooped water into her cupped hands and plunged her face into it, giving her a few moments of relief. In between attempts to cool her skin, she rummaged through the bathroom cupboard in search of the antihistamine tablets Björn took for his hay fever, and swallowed one with some water. When she stood up straight after drinking from the tap she was confronted in the mirror by her own horror-filled gaze, yet the face she saw wasn't hers. It was a raw, red, swollen blob. It was impossible that a cream she'd been using for years could have produced such an extreme allergic reaction.

'Björn!' she cried out helplessly. 'Björn! What did you put in my face cream?'

32

'Maybe I'm trying to get excited over something, simply out of boredom. Maybe it's nothing after all,' Daníel said, distractedly clinking glasses with Áróra.

She had opened a bottle of prosecco, and they'd already made inroads into it while watching Lady Gúgúlú through the living-room window, as she ferried furniture and other household items from her car to the garage apartment.

Daníel had been telling Áróra all about the Kaffikó couple and the feeling he had that they were hiding something. 'It's strange enough that somebody killed their dog. Even stranger that they didn't report it, and yet they did report the damage to their property. I suppose there could be all sorts of reasons for that; still, I don't really hold out much hope of finding anything on them.'

'Don't be so sure of that,' Áróra said, draining her glass and reaching for the bottle to give them a top-up.

'What do you mean?'

'I have the same feeling as you,' she replied. 'There's something fishy about them.'

'What?' Daníel was genuinely curious now.

'Their operating figures don't make sense. I can't put my finger on why that is. But Agla plans to take several random samples from Kaffikó's accounts, as well as those of their competitors, to try to get a clearer picture of what's going on.'

Daníel nodded, thoughtfully. It was at times like this, when Daníel was relaxed, that Áróra found him so handsome she couldn't take her eyes off him. Occasionally he would nudge her and tell her to stop staring, then look embarrassed when she said she was in awe of his beauty. Which was how she felt now. He had on a white T-shirt and a pair of old shorts he used to play basketball in. Áróra sat with his feet in her lap, stroking the soft hair on his legs and gazing at him in profile.

'Marteinn reacted very strangely, so I pressed my advantage and told him I intended to delve deeper into these acts of vandalism. Then he became even more jumpy, and assured me they didn't care about it, that there was no need for me to look into it again. Very odd. The wife sang from the same hymn sheet. They didn't want any action taken about the damage to their property, and they didn't mention the incident with the dog.'

'I can sort of understand that,' Áróra said. 'Don't most people just want the police report for the insurance claim? Or maybe their dog wasn't insured.'

'That occurred to me too. So, I contacted their insurance company, who told me they hadn't made any recent claims for damage to their house or their car. Yet Marteinn told me they'd been compensated.'

'They have plenty of money, of course,' Áróra said, stroking Daníel's leg up to his knee. 'Maybe they didn't want the hassle.'

Daníel nodded. 'Maybe. But still, I have the sense there's more to this than meets the eye. Nothing concrete, just the feeling that they're hiding something. How that might be connected to Europol's money-laundering investigation I don't know. It's more of a hunch than a professional judgement, and it's probably complete nonsense.'

'Or not,' Áróra said, and ran her hand up Daníel's thigh.

'Or not,' he said, and grinned. He looked into Áróra's eyes and he saw her. His mind was on her now, not on the Kaffikó couple. 'What are you thinking?' he asked, his smile broadening.

'I'm thinking how handsome you are,' Áróra replied. 'What a beautiful body you have.'

He laughed. 'So skinny and bony. Wouldn't you prefer a bit more muscle? Surrounded as you always are by bodybuilders.'

Áróra shook her head. 'No. I find muscly men a bit daddyish,' she said. 'Not sexy.'

She picked up her glass from the table, drained it in one gulp and put it down again. Then she grabbed the waistband of Daniel's shorts and began to pull them off him.

WEDNESDAY

33

Ísafold noticed the taxi driver who drove her home from A&E that morning cast furtive glances at her in his rear-view mirror, then look away when their eyes met. She understood his curiosity. She looked like something out of a horror movie. Both the A&E doctor and the dermatologist who was called in had asked her repeatedly about the mask she'd put on her face that had caused this reaction. She replied cagily that it was a 'chemical peel' she'd bought cheaply online. They noted that the redness on her face resembled burns more than any allergy. The fact that she'd washed it off the instant it started to sting meant that only the epidermis had been affected. The doctors said she was fortunate not to have got any of it in her eyes. She'd had a lucky escape. Ísafold promised she'd find the packaging and give them the name of the chemical peel so they could inform the relevant people.

She'd been so scared that night. Björn was pretending to be fast asleep, so she called a taxi and went on her own to A&E. No sooner had she stepped inside and seen the way the people in reception reacted to her than she burst out crying, and the salty tears running down her cheeks had made the burning worse. After receiving what seemed like endless face washes, lotions, sprays and tablets, she was now on her way home with a prescription for painkillers and ointments in her bag, and a follow-up appointment in outpatients in two days' time.

She'd put off calling work until the last minute, and was relieved to find that her boss wasn't there so she was able to leave a message for him. A message saying that unfortunately she had to hand in her notice and wouldn't be coming in to work anymore, and how

sorry she was. She'd have broken down if she'd had to speak to him
in person, so it was better this way. Callous and unjust, but better
given the circumstances. She considered once again whether she
ought to leave Björn. Whether this was the last straw. But she
ended up back in the same place, as always: overwhelmed by a
feeling of emptiness at the thought of being without him. Of course,
Áróra was right when she said their relationship was sick, but then
Áróra had never been in a real relationship. She'd never committed
herself fully to anybody.

The taxi driver did his best not to stare at her when she paid the
fare, and she avoided his eyes so she wouldn't have to see the look of
pity in them. She couldn't bear anyone to show her warmth or sympathy right now. She would only break down and cry, burn her
own cheeks again with her tears.

She felt dizzy as she mounted the stairs and had to cling to the
handrail. Her head felt empty, like a balloon floating in the air,
but at the same time her feet felt leaden and every step was an effort.
When she walked into the apartment she found Björn sitting at the
kitchen table, drinking a cup of coffee and reading the paper.
Without glancing up from the paper, he asked her curtly why she
wasn't at work.

'Do you really think I could go to work at the store looking the
way I do?' she replied sharply, and he frowned at her. First his
mouth fell open as he stared at her, then his lip curled into a sneer.

'God, you're ugly,' he said.

'Yes,' she said. 'And I have you to thank for that. You could've
blinded me.'

'Yeah, yeah,' he said. 'Don't be so melodramatic. You'll be fine.'
His eyes alighted on her handbag. 'Did you get any painkillers?' he
asked and she nodded. He rose to his feet, walked over and took her
bag from her, rummaging inside until he found the prescription
the doctor had written, which she had to fill at the chemist.

'Would you mind getting the ointment I need, too?' she said, *hoping she sounded docile enough for him to do as she asked. She hadn't been able to face stopping off at the chemist on the way home, not looking the way she did, and she and Björn had permission to pick up each other's prescriptions.*

'Hm, I'll do it later, when the lads have gone.' Björn used two boys to run various errands for him and they usually showed up around noon to receive their instructions for the day. Ísafold went out of her way to ignore them, she preferred not to know too much about what Björn was really up to, although she knew it involved buying pills cheaply and selling them at a profit. She assumed it was the boys' job to sell them for him, because somehow Björn always had money, even though he only had a part-time job at a phone shop.

Ísafold went into the bedroom and began to undress. She stretched out the neck on her top so it wouldn't rub against her face when she took it off. Then she pulled out of the drawer a button-down nightshirt that was easy to put on. She was in bed when Björn came in, walked over to his wardrobe and began rifling through his shirts.

'So, are you going to laze about at home, or what?'

'Yes I am, Björn. The doctor told me I needed to rest. I didn't sleep a wink last night. I can hardly go out to find another job looking like this, can I? So much for your brilliant plan.'

'Have you handed in your notice at work?'

'Yes. Wasn't that the idea? Isn't that why you did this to me?'

He wrinkled his nose contemptuously. 'Why the fuck didn't you go on the sick first?' he said, shaking his head. 'You couldn't make an intelligent decision to save your life, Ísafold. It's like whole sections of your brain are missing!'

34

Áróra was waiting outside the Kaffikó on Síðumúli when it opened at seven-thirty. She'd got out of bed in a hurry, before Daníel woke, as she knew if they had coffee together that morning, she was bound to tell him about her visit to Elísabet yesterday, and about Ester Lóa's heart defect. And she knew how that conversation would go. Daníel would scold her for going there, before pointing out to her that aside from any symbolic meaning Ester Lóa's heart defect might have, it was completely irrelevant and had nothing whatsoever to do with reincarnation or with her sister's missing heart. Áróra could tell herself all that, if she only thought about it logically and stopped kidding herself.

She was the first customer of the day, and an aroma of freshly ground coffee enveloped the young barista who smiled amiably as he greeted her.

'What can I get for you today?' he asked, as if she were a regular customer. It must feel welcoming to people who came here often. It created a sense of familiarity, continuity and community.

Áróra looked helplessly at the board above the barista's head, as if she was having difficulty choosing a coffee.

'What do you recommend?' she asked. If she'd drunk coffee that morning with Daníel, she would have started the day with her usual latte, lovingly prepared by him, but now she was feigning indecision to engage the young man in conversation.

'We offer all kinds of coffee: espresso, macchiato, cappuccino, latte, americano, as well as the traditional filter coffee, which is fine if it's made with high-quality beans. The main question is whether you take milk or a milk substitute, and if so how much.

Also, if you'd like any flavourings – syrups or spices. Cinnamon is the most popular, obviously. And finally, if you want to be really nerdy about it, you can choose a darker roast that's more flavourful and has a lower caffeine content, or a lighter roast that's more acidic and is more caffeine rich.'

'Wow!' Áróra said, now more indecisive than ever. 'Why don't you make me a dark-roast coffee with a splash of milk and some exotic spice of your choice.'

The young man laughed. 'Sure,' he said, and began to grapple with the coffee machine. 'Would you like something to eat with it? We have all the traditional pastries.'

Áróra scanned the selection in the glass display case and finally pointed at the happy marriage cake. He cut a slice, put it on a plate and handed it to her.

'Does it get busy here?' she asked.

He shook his head. 'No, this is one of the quieter coffee-houses. Because of the location we don't get many tourists. But some of the other coffeehouses get a lot of them.'

Áróra nodded. 'And is it fun working here?'

He grinned. 'Yeah. It's cool. The owners are nice. We some-times go on out-of-town work weekends, and once a year they send us abroad to learn more about coffee and stuff. It fits in well with school, as the hours are flexible, which means it's easy to work and study at the same time.'

'That's great,' Áróra said, taking her black-pepper macchiato from the young man, who now said goodbye, as another early-bird customer had walked through the door and was demanding his attention.

'What can I get for you today?'

35

Daníel sat at his desk in the police station, gazing out of the window and smiling to himself. His thoughts were still on the night before, and Áróra. It had been a wonderful evening, full of love and laughter, and words the prosecco had helped to coax out and that needed to be said. He sighed contentedly. It would take a lot to upset his mood today.

On the computer screen in front of him was a huge document, which he now turned his attention to, scrolling through it – in search of what, he wasn't entirely sure. Áróra had certainly put a lot of work into her report, even though he'd only asked her to take a peek at Kaffikó's financial data. The lengthy document was a compilation of all the main media coverage the company had received since its launch six years earlier. This comprised interviews with Gyða and Marteinn, a piece about their imports of fairtrade coffee, the recipes handed down to them by their mothers and grandmothers, which they claimed were the inspiration behind their first coffeehouse, as well as pictures and coverage of festive occasions in the history of Kaffikó's coffeehouses, of which there now many.

Daníel paused and scrolled back a bit to a photograph that had drawn his attention. It was from the opening five years ago of Kaffikó's second coffeehouse, and in it he saw Gyða and Marteinn with beaming faces, both with a coffee cup in their hand, and between them stood none other than Sturla Larsen, well-known drug dealer and crime baron. Daníel instantly recognised him, although he'd only seen him twice in person. His style hadn't changed much, though he was thinner; he had the same bleached-blonde straw-like hair Daníel remembered, and sunglasses, even though the photograph was taken indoors. He wasn't named in the caption, which instead stated that the owners were probably toasting the occasion with something stronger than coffee.

Daníel printed out a hard copy of the photograph and studied it closely, as if the printer ink might provide him with the answer the screen couldn't. The answer to how Marteinn and Gyða knew Sturla Larsen. For they clearly knew him well enough to invite him to the opening of their new coffeehouse.

He folded up the printout and slipped it into his breast pocket. He would pop over to Ari Benz with it. It might have some relevance to what Europol was investigating. If he were a lazier cop, or even just a bit more practical, he would await further instructions before delving any deeper into Kaffikó's affairs. Foreign law-enforcement bodies frequently gave the police tip-offs, most of which led nowhere. If this was the case with Marteinn and Gyða, he'd be wasting his time on some wild-goose chase. Still, there was something about the couple that made him want to pursue this – a feeling he'd had since his first meeting with Marteinn, and which Áróra's findings had con-firmed. And seeing them in a photograph with Sturla Larsen did nothing to allay his suspicions.

36

The Canadian Border Services Agency was always very helpful; however, the officer at the other end of the phone heaved a weary sigh when Helena asked for yet another favour.

'You realise that while you're just starting work in Iceland, I'm ending a night shift here,' he said. 'So, I'd advise you not to ask me anything too complicated, as my brain isn't at its freshest right now.'

'We have a video of Björn Árnason leaving Toronto Airport. However, it's taken from a distance and he's wearing a baseball cap, so we can't see his face very clearly. I just want to look at the photograph of him at the border-control gate.'

'We don't have border-control gates in Canada; we have airport kiosks or e-gates. People line up to register to enter the country and a special machine scans their passports.'

'But, the machine takes a picture of the person, right?'

'Yes.'

'And compares it to their passport photograph?'

'No. It doesn't, actually. And I doubt your border-control gates do either.'

'Really?' This was news to Helena. 'So why take a photo of people when they enter the country?'

'Over here – and I can only speak for the Canadian Border Services Agency – we do so for two reasons: firstly, so the machines can compare them with a list of photographs of wanted people, to check whether the individual is a known terrorist or criminal.'

'And the other reason?'

'It's to help us respond to questions asked by folk like yourself.'

Helena had walked straight into the man's trap, and she had to laugh. Still, she found the information concerning.

'Are you telling me anyone can wave a passport in the air with somebody else's photo in it and enter the country just like that?'

'Yes. Or rather, the passports are checked. Our machines x-ray them to check they're not false, and alert us if they are. But in theory, if you're entering Canada for the first time with a valid passport that belongs to someone else, then the answer is yes.'

Helena felt mildly relieved to know that Iceland wasn't the only country with leaky borders and a computer system that seemed designed more for show and to offer people a false sense of security.

'I'd be grateful if you could send me the photo of Björn Árnason when he entered Canada.'

'It might take me a few minutes to find it. I'll send it to you later by email. Always happy to be of service to our colleagues over there in Iceland.'

Helena thanked the man and hung up. She stood and paced once around the room. Both to stretch her legs but also to kill time while she waited for the email with the photograph that could either prove or disprove the theory she'd concocted in her head.

37

Felix awoke so hungry his stomach hurt. He hadn't dared venture out the evening before to get himself something to eat. The bag with the money had thrown him completely. He was afraid to let it out of his sight, but at the same time too terrified to take it with him, even if he was only going to look for a hotdog stand. In addition, he'd had difficulty falling asleep. He'd thought he heard all manner of noises that his tired brain interpreted as threats to the bag as well as to himself. The growl of a motorboat out in the fjord sounded like a car approaching, and the creak of floorboards somewhere in the house like someone sneaking around just outside his bedroom door. This had resulted in him leaping to his feet every five minutes to move the bag. He'd locked it in the wardrobe, but then realised, just as he was about to drop off, that this was the first place someone would look. He got out of bed and carried the bag into the bathroom, where he wrapped it in a towel and hid it behind the shower curtain. Next he slid it under the bed. And now he'd woken with it in his arms. Embracing it as he might an adored lover.

The dawn light seeped in through the window, making his fears of the previous night seem ridiculous – although not entirely. Maybe he was right to feel more nervous – more fearful about there being money in the bag rather than pills. Only addicts would kill to get their hands on a stash of drugs. But money was different. Everyone wanted money.

Felix got to his feet and took the bag with him into the bathroom. He locked the door, urinated, rinsed out his mouth then stood under the shower and let the hot water flow over his head briefly. He felt better than he had last night, but was still anxious at the thought of leaving the guest house. What if someone had got wind of his trip? What if the old lady in reception was untrustworthy? Did she know what was in the bag? Could she have told someone? Who had brought the bag on the ferry and left it in the room, and had they been followed? He tried to take a few deep breaths then lowered the thermostat on the shower to cold. He groaned and felt his stomach contract, but it had the desired effect. His head felt clearer, and as he rubbed himself dry with trembling hands he reproached himself for being such a coward. He was man enough to look after the money. If Sturla had thought there was any real danger involved, he would never have sent him to fetch it alone.

He pulled on his clothes, grabbed the bag and raced down the stairs. Two innocent-looking tourists were sitting at the breakfast table, chatting in hushed voices in an unfamiliar language he thought might be Hungarian or Finnish. They didn't seem at all interested in him or the bag, and the old lady was nowhere to be seen. He grabbed a couple of boiled eggs and a cheese straw from the buffet table, stuffed them in his jacket pocket, resting the bag on his feet while he poured some coffee into a paper cup. Then he nodded to the two tourists and made a hasty departure.

On his way to the car, Felix glanced about. There was no one around, though the town was clearly awake, with the accompanying commotion coming from the harbour. He climbed into the driver's seat and pressed the central door lock. Then he stowed the bag in the footwell of the front passenger seat and put his coffee into the cup holder between the seats.

He was halfway to Fjarðarheiði mountain pass before he felt relaxed enough to take the cheese straw out of his pocket and bite into it. He saw nothing unusual in the rear-view mirror. He had left the two small rental cars that crawled out of town after him far below. He stepped on the accelerator, and enjoyed being thrown back in his seat by the momentum. The Audi took off like a rocket, handling with ease the steep ascent from the fjord. He experienced again the flash of joy he'd felt when he set out yesterday, and that feeling eased somewhat the weight of responsibility.

38

Helena didn't need to wait long, because the instant she checked her email the message popped into her inbox. She gave a disappointed sigh. It seemed that two years ago the Canadian Services Agency had changed their computer system. All the data on the old system had been saved but then subsequently lost. She was about to close her email when she read the officer's sign-off message and saw that he'd added: 'P.S. Check the attachment.'

Helena instantly clicked on the attachment, which took a while to open. She felt like hitting the computer to make it work faster. Finally the image came up on the screen. She studied it closely. It was the scanned image of a document – a mostly blank page with a few lines printed at the top. She had to zoom in to decipher the letters. She read it several times before fully understanding the context; it was a four-year-old report entry by the Canadian Border Services Agency stating that, as requested by the Icelandic police, they had sent a photograph of Björn Árnason entering Canada.

She read it through once more. There was no mention of how the photograph had been sent, or to whom. Helena whistled and waved to Vala, who sat absorbed in her phone on the far side of the room. Noticing Helena, she gave a start and came running over.

'Take a look at this,' Helena said, pointing at the screen.

Vala leaned over her to read the tiny writing, resting her hand on Helena's shoulder to steady herself. Helena could feel the heat from Vala's hand through her shirt as she became immersed in the cloud of fragrance enveloping the young woman.

She spun round and rose from her chair. 'Sit here,' she said, 'so you can read it properly.'

Vala studied the screen for a few moments then shook her head. 'Does this mean they already sent us the photograph we just asked them for?'

'Exactly,' Helena replied. 'What we don't know is how, or to whom they sent it. Every piece of information we receive regarding a case should be entered in the database, but that photograph isn't there.'

'At any rate, we haven't found it. Do you want me to search through all the case files? Perhaps it was incorrectly labelled or something?'

Helena looked at her for a moment, to be sure she wasn't joking. Then she felt a wave of sympathy. Vala was so young. Not that long ago Helena had been in the same position herself, full of energy and convinced her unstinting hard work would earn her plaudits and achieve results. Sympathy aside, she wasn't about to refuse Vala's offer to put in the hours of mind-numbing work it would take to wade through the archive in search of the photograph.

'That's great, if you can take it on,' Helena said. 'I'll talk to everyone who worked on the original team to see if any of them remembers the photograph.'

'Maybe they sent it by fax and it's languishing in the archives somewhere?' Vala called out playfully to Helena, as she headed for the door.

'It was only four years ago, Vala, dear,' Helena retorted, but Vala's remark had given her another idea. She was fairly certain the photograph wouldn't have been faxed, so maybe someone on the team received it in an email and forgot to upload it onto the database.

She bounded down the police station steps two by two and shot across the road to Hlemmur. She wasn't sure how many of her colleagues she'd have to talk to about this, but four of them had worked on the original missing-person case, and as time went on that number had increased.

'Eight cinnamon buns, please,' she said to the woman behind the counter at Hlemmur, who instantly began placing them into a bag. Helena's mouth watered just looking at them, but she mustn't give in to temptation. On this occasion the buns were currency.

39

The manager at the assisted-living apartments for the elderly on Lindargata had said she would give her a call that afternoon, but Ísafold knew this was a mere formality. She had presented well in the interview and was confident she'd get the job. She'd explained she was recovering from a skin condition, and her face was proof of this: her skin was still flaking, revealing the new, raw, pink skin underneath, as she didn't want to irritate it by wearing make-up. The story of her ailment gave her an excuse to say she hadn't been on the job market for a while, as she didn't want to have to ask the store for a reference, following her sudden departure. She also told her prospective new employers that she wanted to work with people, as Björn had told her to.

Relations had been tense between her and Björn following the burns she received to her face. He hadn't admitted to putting anything in her cream, and therefore hadn't apologised. He was distant and cold with her, but somehow this time she didn't care, because she still felt angry. Not angry enough to leave him, though, not angry enough to have told anyone what he did to her, because deep down, she was aware that other people's reactions often affected the way she saw things. Áróra and Grímur and Ebbi always became angry on her behalf, used the words 'violence' and 'bullying', but this was because they didn't understand her and Björn's relationship. They didn't understand this world that only the two of them belonged in, and which, yes, could be harsh at times, but was also full of love and more passionate than anyone else could comprehend.

She alighted from the bus at Mjóddin shopping centre and began walking up the hill. She considered stopping off at the hardware store to buy some filler to try to fix the hole Björn had kicked in the kitchen unit. But as she approached the store, a family emerged, their trolley full of gardening supplies and summer plants, and somehow the sight of them filled her with sorrow. Something about the parents and their two daughters took her back to her and Áróra's childhood. The girls were bouncing around their parents, who had that expectant look some people get when they're embarking on a project. It was often like that with her mum and dad: planning work on the garden, or painting the kids' bedrooms or varnishing the kitchen cupboards, and the whole family participated, so that gradually the house belonged to all of them, each able to see their own handiwork in every room.

Ísafold swallowed the lump rising in her throat, turned away from the store and decided to go straight home. It flashed through her mind that she and Björn would never work together making improvements to their apartment. Up until now, it had been Björn who destroyed things and she did her best to fix the damage.

The door to the apartment stood open as she reached the top of the stairs, and Björn's errand boys were on their way out. He patted them cheerfully on the shoulders, and ruffled the hair on one of their heads.

'My man Felix here is a genius and a prince!' he said, and the boys laughed. Then he grabbed Ísafold's hand and pulled her to him. 'Come here, sweetheart.' He kissed her on the neck, and she felt the pleasure that coursed through her body at his touch mingle with the hope that seemed to reawaken in her heart for the slightest of reasons: the merest caress from Björn, a faint smile, a hint of tenderness. She longed for nothing more than to be Björn's sweetheart. She only wished it wasn't so painful.

40

It wasn't even midday by the time Áróra finished visiting the five Kaffikó coffeehouses closest to downtown Reykjavík. She had sampled five different coffees – the last two being decaffs – and rather than drink them on the premises, had asked for a take-away cup and poured half the contents down the gutter between coffeehouses. But the coffees were excellent, and she'd also sampled their pastries, which she had to admit were all delicious too. She had chatted with the staff working at the different branches, who all spoke well of the owners, praised the training they received and said that Gyða and Marteinn were flexible about rearranging shifts if something came up, and this was why they managed to hold on to such good people. Everyone Áróra spoke to had been working for Kaffikó for a while, the majority for more than two years – longer than the average for catering jobs in Iceland. But what Áróra found most interesting was that they all said it was quiet at their coffeehouse while the others were busy due to tourists.

Áróra sat in her car, holding her last half-cup of coffee. Spread before her was the map where she'd marked the various Kaffikó locations. She considered which of the coffeehouses might be the busy ones. She'd visited all those it was possible to walk to from downtown, and had difficulty believing the other coffee-houses further out, in Smárahvammur or on Reykjavíkurvegur in Hafnarfjörður could be more popular with tourists. It was a complete mystery. Or maybe it wasn't. Maybe this was what Kaffikó's staff was led to believe: that the other coffeehouses were busier, but without specifying which. Maybe this was a nar-rative promoted within the company and in the media, when in fact none of Kaffikó's coffeehouses were particularly popular, as they were located in relatively quiet, less prosperous areas of the city. But then the revenues must come from some other source.

It would be interesting to look over the random samples Agla was going to provide her with. Áróra was convinced that when she compared Kaffikó's accounts with those of its competitors, she would find significant discrepancies in both the expenses and the income columns. There had to be a reason why Kaffikó's profits were so much bigger than those of the other coffeehouses, and it was pretty obvious it had nothing to do with tourism.

Absorbed in her own thoughts, Áróra gave a start when her phone rang, and a spurt of coffee leapt from her cup onto the map. Leaning forward to reach for a napkin in the glove compartment, she spilled even more coffee over the map.

'Shit!'

'I think I deserve a better name after last night.' Daníel's voice came through the loudspeaker, which had automatically paired with her phone.

'Oh, fuck. Sorry. I just spilled something.'

'I was wondering whether you'd like to meet me for a coffee?' Daníel said, and Áróra groaned.

'Ugh. I think I've had enough coffees for one day.'

'How about dinner, then?' Daníel asked.

'Sounds good to me. Why not come over to mine this evening. I'll buy some sushi.'

41

Oxycontin, OxyNorm Dispersa, Sobril, sleeping pills, fentanyl, Vicodin, codeine. All the residents at the assisted-living apartments were prescribed one or more of these drugs, and Björn seemed to have known and anticipated this. Ísafold quickly realised this was the reason why he'd been so keen for her to give up her job at the shopping centre and work with elderly folk. During her first week there, Björn had told her to bring home one blister strip of pills after her shift, but today he wanted four.

'Hello?' Ísafold called out as she entered the apartment. The man who lived there was in his late eighties, and every day for the past week he'd been telling Ísafold the story of his life in chapters. Among other things he'd confided in her that since his wife died, he'd been taking a sleeping pill every night. Ísafold's job was to carry out a so-called morning check-in, which meant washing the dishes, taking out rubbish, running a damp cloth over the toilet and wash basin and in this case helping the old boy out of bed. She also had to massage cream into his dry, cracked feet and help him on with his trousers. He was able to button up his shirt and tie his own tie; he told her he never left the house without a necktie.

'Hello, dear!' he called out to her. 'I'm just lying here listening to the radio.'

'I'll wash my hands and be with you in a jiffy,' Ísafold called back, as she hurried into the kitchen nook and turned on the tap. While the water was running, she opened the biscuit tin on the kitchen table, from which, the previous Friday, he had asked her to fetch his medicine, and she prayed to a higher power that he hadn't decided to keep them next to his bed, like some of the other residents. She thought she'd hit the jackpot when she found a box containing 7.5 mg of Imovane. Björn would be pleased with that.

It was one of the drugs he said sold for a good price. Removing a strip from the box, she stuffed it into her pocket then turned off the tap.

The old man beamed as she appeared in the doorway, and Ísafold felt a surge of guilt and her eyes welled up. Had she really been reduced to this? Stealing from the elderly who trusted her with their health and welcomed her into their homes? She forced a smile, gave a sniff, and recalled Björn's speech about how it was fine to take drugs off old people, who often didn't recall whether or not they'd taken their medication, and in any case GPs wrote out endless prescriptions for them, as no one was concerned about addiction among the elderly.

Ísafold put on a pair of latex gloves, dipped her fingers into the pot of cream and began massaging the old man's feet.

'You have such a gentle touch, my dear,' he said. 'You should study to become a nurse. You'd make an excellent one.'

Ísafold smiled then quickly averted her eyes and gave another sniff. She'd never be able to learn anything. Let alone something as complicated as nursing. Björn was right. She wasn't the sharpest knife in the drawer.

After she'd finished cleaning, had taken out the rubbish and said goodbye to the old man, who whistled to himself as he tied his necktie, she went into the next flat, where she played the same game with the tap, but found no pills in the kitchen. The couple who lived here kept theirs either by their beds or in the bathroom. She said good morning as she entered their bedroom, and the couple replied as one. The husband was able to get out of bed on his own, but his wife was arthritic and needed help both getting up and getting dressed. The woman sat on the edge of the bed, and Ísafold glanced about the bedroom while kneeling in front of her and pulling up each of her trouser legs. The two bedside tables were covered in clutter, which seemed the rule rather than the exception with the elderly, but she saw no sign of any pills among the water bottles, napkins, books, mobile phones and chargers. She felt mildly relieved, as though somehow not seeing any drugs absolved her from having to steal them. But then another feeling took over. Fear. Björn would be less than pleased if she didn't bring home four blister strips like he'd told her to.

'May I use your toilet quickly?' she asked the woman, after helping her to her feet. 'I'm bursting to go.'

'Of course, my dear,' the woman said. 'Be my guest.'

Ísafold gave a quick smile then hurried into the bathroom and locked the door behind her. Facing her on the wall was a large drugs cabinet with a key in the lock. She opened it and heaved a sigh of relief. It contained such a treasure trove of painkillers, she could easily swipe two or three strips from the various boxes.

42

Helena had started with Daníel, who deduced from the size of the bag that she had plenty of cinnamon buns and demanded two. In contrast, Kristján had been more malleable and accepted one in exchange for the favour. Now it was Palli's turn. He had his headphones on and was absorbed in whatever it was he was doing.

'What do you want?' he asked suspiciously, when he saw Helena approach his desk waving a cinnamon bun in front of him.

'I need to ask you to search in your messages for an email ending *gc.ca*,' Helena said, smiling as sweetly as she could.

'What's that? Canada?'

'Yes. I need to see all emails from the Canadian Border Services Agency.'

'Why?'

'They claim they sent us a photograph ages ago of Björn Árnason passing through the entry gate into Canada. Except that it's not in our database.'

Palli looked even more suspicious, and squirmed in his chair. 'And what makes you think I might have it?'

'I don't think anything,' Helena said. 'I'm asking everyone who was on the original investigation team.'

Palli grunted, still eyeing her with mistrust.

'I'll give you two cinnamon buns,' Helena said, temptingly.

Palli turned his nose up at the offer, and began typing on his keyboard. Helena stood behind him to peer over his shoulder at the screen, and while she was waiting for him to find what she was looking for, she wondered under what circumstances she might place her hand on Palli's shoulder, the way Vala had done with her earlier. She hadn't reached a conclusion before Palli pulled up a list of emails he'd received from the Canadian Border Services Agency some four years earlier.

'Would you mind opening them all to check for attachments?' she asked.

Palli sighed reluctantly but did as she requested. The first email contained the video of Björn leaving the airport, hunched over, wearing a baseball cap, his face in shadow. This video was in the database and Helena had seen it several times. The next email, however, contained a photo attachment.

'Click on it,' Helena said, and when the file opened, she nearly howled with joy.

'What is it?' asked Palli.

'It's the photograph!' Helena cried. 'The missing photograph that isn't in the database.'

'Okay, I'm sorry, I forgot to upload it,' Palli said with a hint of irritation. 'But we received confirmation that Björn travelled to Canada after Ísafold disappeared, so what difference does the photograph make?'

'It makes all the difference,' Helena said, raising her voice unintentionally. 'Because the man in the photo isn't Björn!'

Palli looked at her in disbelief, grimaced and inspected the image. 'Really? Are you sure?' He went into the database, pulled up a head shot of Björn and placed the two images side by side. 'To me they look like the same guy,' he said.

But Helena knew she was right. The theory she'd been formulating in her head was correct. She had the evidence. The man leaving the airport in Toronto wasn't Björn. The facial image taken at the Canadian entry gate showed unmistakeably that it was Ómar, Olga's young friend, who now called himself Snæþór Ómar.

43

The random accounting samples Agla had requested from the three coffeehouse chains certainly made interesting reading. Daníel had asked Áróra to look into Kaffikó all the way back to its beginnings, and here she was, with three boxes of files in front of her containing accounting folders from all three companies dating back seven years. It was a relief to have a big project to work on, and hoped it would take up most of her day, for whenever her mind sat idle that searing pain would assail her, and she'd start to think about Ísafold.

She began to sift through the boxes, placing to one side the data belonging to Kaffikó's two main competitors. If their annual financial reports were anything to go by, she'd find nothing of interest in their accounts. Both companies had started off small, built their brands slowly, and made no profits to speak of during the first ten years or so. Kaffikó was a different matter. As they never tired of telling the media, when Gyða and Marteinn founded their company six years ago they'd mortgaged everything they owned, and in its first year of operation, Kaffikó's first and only coffeehouse had incurred huge losses. So huge, in fact, it was surprising they didn't file for bankruptcy.

Yet immediately afterwards, they opened a second coffeehouse, however, Áróra didn't need to go through their accounts to understand how that came about; she'd already found the explanation in their annual financial report dating back five years. According to these, Gyða and Marteinn had sold almost half of the share capital in Kaffikó Ltd., and had invested the money back into the business. Nor did it take her long to discover the identity of the new shareholder, who was registered as a private individual, not a holding company. A man she'd never heard of, and whom she couldn't identify as belonging to the group of well-known investors.

Most significantly of all, though, was that no sooner had the new investor been brought on board and the second coffeehouse opened, than the company started to thrive. Suddenly both coffeehouses were showing a profit. A huge profit. Áróra rummaged in the box and pulled out the file covering the company's first two years. The figures showed unequivocally that between year one and year two, Kaffikó's revenue had risen considerably, although in itself this wasn't necessarily unusual; both coffeehouses had clearly grown in popularity after the second one opened, the business thrived and soon they were opening new branches all over Reykjavík.

It wasn't uncommon for a new investor to bring a different dynamic or a fresh direction to a business, and sometimes even a new client base, although that didn't seem to be the case with Kaffikó's investor. As far as Áróra could see, he was what was known as a silent partner. He didn't have a seat on the board of directors, nor did he appear to be a spokesman for Kaffikó and he didn't participate actively in any of the company's media coverage. He did, however, receive a handsome return on his investment. The accounts also showed he was on Kaffikó's payroll, and received a generous salary as well as the use of a company car, although nowhere did it specify what his role was.

After searching vainly through the company directory, Áróra was no closer to knowing who this Sturla person was or where he'd come from. He didn't appear to have owned any companies previously, and hadn't sold a business to finance the purchase of his stake in Kaffikó. It was as if he'd literally fallen from the sky, with his pockets full of money.

Áróra's fingers almost tingled with excitement when she opened the first file containing receipts from the coffee shops' daily takings. She flipped through them eagerly until she found the first bundle neatly stapled to its corresponding bank deposit slip. She made a note of the amounts and turned to the next printout. At a glance it was exactly as she'd suspected. To be absolutely sure, though, she'd need to go through several months' worth of accounts.

44

The team meeting with Gutti, Baldvin, Kristján and Palli was rather uninspiring. It was as if all the energy had been sucked out of them. This was often the case when an investigation had ground to a halt and the possibilities had dwindled. Helena sat next to Gutti, and on the other side of him Vala, who seemed to be the only one wide awake and tirelessly taking notes.

'Well, guys, we're not making much progress, but we won't give up. We'll keep crossing off items on our to-do list, and if in the next two or three weeks no new leads emerge, the commissioner has said there's a chance we may get some assistance from foreign experts in cold cases to review the data and assess what might be worth revisiting.' Gutti looked forlornly at the team, who barely responded – except for Vala who nodded assiduously.

'Kristján and Palli, I understand you spoke to Björn's colleagues again, correct?' said Gutti.

'Yeah,' replied Kristján. 'They seemed to think he was an okay guy, but as he only worked part-time, nobody knew him very well and he was considered as a kind of casual worker. He was a good salesman and customers seemed happy with his service.' This appeared to match what the old reports had said.

'Baldvin, your job was to ask around Ísafold's former places of work?'

'Yes, that's right. We spoke to her boss and colleagues, but they had nothing new to add to what was in the reports back when Daníel and the others worked the case. Ísafold frequently came to work with bruises and other visible injuries from beatings. She downplayed them, claimed she'd tripped over, walked into a door, that kind of thing. Not long before she disappeared, she was sacked from her job at the assisted-living apartments for the elderly on the grounds she was stealing pills from the residents. The manager wasn't sure whether they were for her personal use, but said she didn't have the impression Ísafold was an addict.'

'Okay. The neighbours. That was your job, right girls?' It never ceased to get on Helena's nerves the way male bosses seemed to view more than one woman as a group and address them as 'girls' rather than by their first names. Still, she sat up in her chair and smiled politely.

'Yes, that's right. My name's Helena and this is Vala, our trainee officer, whom you all know.'

Gutti looked at her, puzzled. 'Yes, we all know each other here, so there's no need for introductions,' he said.

Helena grinned. 'I'm glad to hear it. Okay, two of the neighbours living in the block when Ísafold and Björn disappeared are still there, and they're the only two who had any contact with the couple, although not a lot. Olga, who lives in the apartment opposite theirs, is currently on holiday in Canada and isn't picking up our calls. She may have switched her phone off. However, I have to say, their downstairs neighbour, Grímur, came out with some interesting information that wasn't in the original report.'

'Really?'

'Yes, he told us Björn was dealing drugs and had a group of young lads running errands for him. They sold the pills he bought cheaply from elderly people or had Ísafold steal from her place of work. This explains why he could afford to work only part-time.'

'We already know that,' Gutti cut in, but Helena raised a finger to indicate that wasn't all.

'Grímur also told us another interesting fact that we didn't know. One of the lads Björn introduced to drugs was Olga's son.

He became heavily addicted and died not long after from an overdose. This gives Olga a motive to resent Björn.'

'But hardly Ísafold?' Palli put in. 'Why would Olga resent Ísafold for something Björn did?'

'True. Something else got me thinking, though, and that's the connection they all have with Canada. Olga makes frequent trips there, and when Björn disappeared it was believed he'd gone to Canada. This struck me as peculiar, so I got in touch with the Canadian Border Service Agency, hoping they might be able to provide us with a photograph of Björn taken at the entry gate, or more precisely of the person carrying his passport, because, as you can see here,' she said, pulling a printout of the facial image from her folder and placing it in the middle of the table, 'the man in this photograph isn't Björn at all.'

A murmur went round the team, and a couple of them sat up in their chairs. While Gutti inspected the photograph, Helena saw out of the corner of her eye Palli sink down in his seat. She had no intention of reporting him for this. Raking up past mistakes was bad for morale. She would let everyone think the Canadians had only just sent them the photograph. And it wouldn't hurt to have Palli owe her, she thought. This, she reflected, was how you won the favour of others in the team. By standing together and helping each other out.

'I assume you've found out who this is?' Gutti asked, waving the photograph as he might a fan.

'Yes,' said Helena. 'We think the young man's real name is Ómar Farki. He sought asylum here in Iceland, and lived with Olga for a time while he was waiting for his application to be processed. After his claim was rejected he went to live in Canada, where Olga visits him regularly. He calls himself Snæþór Ómar on Facebook, and although we can't be sure he goes by that name in his daily life in Canada, the name itself, as well as his friendship with Olga, shows he has a connection to Iceland. I'm not suggesting he and Olga murdered Björn for his passport, but this is certainly interesting, isn't it?'

Gutti scratched his head pensively. 'Well, well, well,' he muttered. 'Well, well, well.'

All eyes in the room were trained on Gutti, waiting for him to say something else. However, he simply continued to stare at the photograph, and the cheers and praise Helena had been half expecting didn't materialise.

'Shall I ask the Canadian Border Services Agency if they'll work with us to try to find Olga and Ómar?' she asked.

Gutti shook his head. 'No, as head of the team, that's my job. Baldvin, you can assist me on this. It needs looking into straight away.'

Helena wanted to protest that Gutti didn't choose her to work with him on this, seeing as how she was the one who had supplied what, to judge from his expression, was a significant lead.

But Gutti quickly moved on. 'The rest of you continue crossing things off the to-do list.' He glanced at the board behind him. 'Björn's girlfriend, the one he took up with after Ísafold disappeared. Nothing came out of our interview with her back then, but we could speak to her again, see if we can't jog her memory.' Helena put her hand up to volunteer for the task, but Gutti pointed to Kristján then carried on. 'We also need to talk to Narcotics about whether Björn might have had some connection with the criminal underworld or whether he was just a small-time dealer selling stolen medication.' Once again, Helena's hand shot up but Gutti assigned the task to Baldvin. 'And then there's the police log from Suðurnes covering the period from when Ísafold disappeared until Björn disappeared. There's nothing of interest on the database from that time, so we'll need to check those logbooks.'

The other team members looked away, leaning over their

notes to try to make themselves small. No one wanted to carry out tedious computer work that would almost certainly give no results.

Gutti looked searchingly at the company.

'You girls can get cracking on that,' he said.

There was something about the knock that made Ísafold's stomach tighten into a knot. She instantly knew that whoever was banging on her door didn't mean well. It couldn't be Björn as he had a key, and anyway that wasn't his knock. Nor could it be Ómar, because rather than knock, he scratched at the door, as though half hoping no one would hear.

This person's knock was calm but persistent, as if it announced serious trouble. Ísafold's first thought was that it might be the police, and she rushed into the kitchen, grabbed the two strips of pills she'd brought home from work and stuffed them into a drawer.

As soon as she opened the door a man walked in whose domineering presence made Ísafold recoil instinctively. He was tall, and not so much blonde as yellow-haired, as if the bleach he'd used wasn't strong enough and his natural colour showed through. Following on his heels were two sinewy-looking young men in tracksuits with nasty sneers on their faces.

'Yes, hello?' Ísafold said as if she were answering a phone call.

The man narrowed his eyes and stared straight at her. He was dressed in a dark-blue suit with a pale T-shirt underneath and white trainers, so new they almost glowed. Around his neck hung a gold chain that accentuated the yellow sheen in his hair.

'I'm here to see your boyfriend,' the man said presently, and Ísafold managed to murmur that Björn wasn't at home.

The yellow-haired man jerked his head, with which the other two men instantly began combing the apartment. One of them searched in the bathroom and the kitchen, while Ísafold heard the other fling open the bedroom door. They came back both shaking their heads and wearing immutable expressions, as if they'd done the exact same thing a hundred times that day and *bursting into people's homes to look for them was a part of their everyday grind.*

Ísafold's heart sank to the pit of her stomach when the man with yellow hair took a step towards her. His face felt alarmingly close, and when she automatically recoiled, she collided with one of the young men now standing directly behind her, so that she could feel his breath on her hair.

'My name's Sturla and I'm not happy,' the yellow-haired man said, talking through gritted teeth, as if the tension in his body was so great, he was about to break his molars.

Ísafold nodded, or at least she thought she nodded – she wasn't sure whether she'd actually moved, as a kind of numbness or paralysis seemed to have overtaken her.

'And now I've come to collect the money your lowlife boyfriend owes me,' the man continued. 'He's been poaching on my territory in a big way, and worse still, he's undercutting me.'

Ísafold stood as though petrified, too afraid to move and unsure whether anything she might say would placate this man or make matters worse. She wasn't completely sure what this Sturla person was referring to, although she suspected it had something to do with the pills, and Felix's and Mummi's errands. Before she could think of something to say that might calm the men down, or make them leave, Sturla lost his patience and took a step closer.

'What are you waiting for, woman?!' he yelled in her face. At which her vocal cords jumped to attention and emitted a shrill whimper. The two young men laughed, and she thought she saw Sturla's lip curve into a smile. 'Go and get my money before I have to shake it out of you.'

'I don't know anything about any money...' she groaned, and now her legs turned to jelly and her knees buckled so that she fell backward into the arms of the young man standing behind her. He hoisted her back into an upright position and she felt herself sway on her feet.

'He must keep his cash somewhere,' Sturla said.

Ísafold shook her head. 'He'd never tell me where,' she replied.

Sturla snorted. 'No. I can well believe that. He's the mean-spirited type. Probably always afraid for himself. Probably always shitting himself, huh?'

Ísafold nodded in agreement, even though the truth was she was the one who was always shit-scared. For all she knew, Björn was never afraid of anything.

'Tell Björn no one gets to deal on my patch without me getting my share. Am I right in thinking he's been doing this for some time, even though I've only been made aware of it recently?'

Ísafold shrugged. She genuinely didn't know the answer. 'It must only be small amounts,' she said, aware of how pathetic her voice sounded.

The man seemed to notice, too, and he softened. He stepped back and glanced about him with an expression that was verging on friendly.

'I will collect what he owes me. By fair means or foul,' he added, sounding now like a stern schoolteacher.

Ísafold nodded vigorously. Then she remembered the pills. Björn had told her that four strips were the equivalent of a month's salary for her, so two strips must be worth something. Maybe it would help if she let the man have the two she'd brought home with her that day.

'I have some pills,' she said. 'You could take them as part payment of the debt.'

She darted into the kitchen, and the youth who followed close behind snatched the blister strips from her as she retrieved them from the drawer. He snorted and handed them to Sturla, who took them and turned them over in his hands.

'It's oxy and codeine,' Ísafold said brightly, but Sturla merely gazed at her with a look of pity.

'All right, my friend,' he said. He stuffed the strips into his pocket, and gestured to the two youths to leave.

They obeyed his command without hesitation and posted themselves in the hallway, like trained soldiers.

Reaching forward, Sturla clasped Ísafold by the chin and pushed her head back. Then he stared into her eyes and whispered: 'Tell Björn to contact me. And to make it quick. I'll add a daily fine for each day he doesn't pay what he owes me. Understood?'

Unable to nod while he was clasping her chin, Ísafold managed to croak:

'Okay, I'll tell him.'

46

Felix would have loved to test the Audi's top speed, but instead he set the cruise control and limited himself to coasting at a hundred kilometres per hour. It would be awkward if the police stopped him with the bag in the car. He'd noticed several cars on his tail, some he'd outrun, others overtook him, but none appeared to be following him. Upon reaching the sands south of Skaftafell, he turned onto a side road alongside a protective barrier and got out of the car to relieve himself. It felt good to be alone out in the wilderness, the black sands stretching endlessly in three directions, and no sound save the occasional cries of moorland birds he couldn't name.

He felt terribly hungry as he turned back onto the main road and continued to drive – the mighty Vatnajökull glacier on his right, its interminable whiteness ever-present like some fact of life, no matter how long he drove. Although his view of the highest peak, Hvannadalshnjúkur, became gradually distorted the further west he went.

Felix couldn't help sneaking the odd glance at the bag lying next to him in the passenger footwell, as though half expecting it might stir from its spot, like a living animal waiting for the chance to escape from him. He tightened his grip on the wheel, glanced in the rear-view mirror and thought he spotted the outline of a black car following him, but when he looked again, he realised it was an optical illusion, in fact it was the back of a rental car that had passed him a moment ago and was now speeding away from him in the other direction.

Vatnajökull was behind him and he was approaching Mýrdalsjökull when his hunger became unbearable. He felt he could have eaten a horse. Images of hamburgers in soft buns danced

before his eyes, oozing tomato sauce and pickle; hotdogs sla-
thered in remoulade sauce and topped with crispy fried onion;
toasted ham and cheese sandwiches fresh from the grill with
melted cheese dripping from the sides. French fries with mayo
ketchup. A Prince Polo chocolate wafer and a can of Coke, or
maybe a malt soda with orangeade, or one of each so he could
sip them alternately and allow his mind to wander back to the
Christmases spent at his grandma's house. He swallowed saliva
a few times, and his hunger abated long enough for him to avoid
being tempted to stop off at Vík. He sped past the town, and
continued heading west into the endless blackness.

He gave in as he approached Hvolsvöllur. Hunger was by now
gnawing at his insides. He had to eat something soon, or he'd
pass out at the wheel. And Hvolsvöllur wasn't a bad place to
stop. The town didn't attract many tourists, so he should get
served quickly, and if he was lucky maybe the convenience store
had a drive-thru. He clung to this thought, convincing himself
there was a drive-thru at the convenience store. But when he
arrived, it turned out to be a false memory. He'd have to go into
the store to buy food. He was on the edge of abandoning his
plan, but his stomach ached from hunger and he felt sick. He
needed to eat something. There were few people in the store, so
with any luck he'd be served quickly, but what he couldn't decide
was whether he should take the bag with him or leave it in the
car. After persuading himself he'd look more conspicuous if he
took it inside with him, he decided to leave it lying in the footwell, like any ordinary sports bag. Anyone peering in through
the window would assume it contained sweaty clothes and
smelly trainers. In addition, the store had a glass frontage so he
could see the car from the counter.

He locked the car, entered the store and stood in the queue.
While he waited to be served, he turned to face the window so
as to keep an eye on the car. The aroma of grilled meat wafting

through the convenience store made Felix even hungrier, and he wanted to hurry the two girls in front of him, who seemed unable to decide what they wanted and were chatting about it as if they had all day. When Felix's turn came, after what felt like an eternity, he ordered two cheeseburgers, a Coke, a packet of chocolate corn puffs and a liquorice roll, then positioned himself over by the window while he waited for his food.

He didn't have to wait long and, with a sigh of relief, he grabbed the paper carrier in one hand and the cup of Coke in the other, then asked for a straw so he wouldn't spill any of it in the car, and hurried out. The smell from the bag made Felix's mouth water, and he couldn't wait to sink his teeth into the soft burger bun. He unlocked the car and slipped into the front seat, but when he set the paper carrier on the passenger seat what he saw made his hand go suddenly limp, and he dropped the Coke in his lap. He felt as if his heart had sunk to the pit of his stomach and he gave a cry of horror. The passenger footwell was empty.

The bag was gone.

47

Áróra exuded confidence as she stood in the middle of her living room and pointed, like a somewhat excited professor, at the whiteboard she'd erected and which was covered in scrawl. Daniel's first response when he entered the room was to laugh at the scene before him. The delicious sushi dinner Áróra had bought for them was still in its packaging, and she'd clearly just dumped it on the table, being far more interested in setting up her mini lecture theatre, which included a projector she'd hooked up to her computer. On the whiteboard she'd drawn a diagram explaining how Kaffikó engaged in money-laundering.

'Kaffikó employs a shift manager, who is usually the most experienced member of staff, and works with one or two others. It's a common enough arrangement in a business of this kind. What's unusual about Kaffikó, though, is that the shift managers aren't responsible for cashing up. And, according to what I've been able to find out, that extends to the cashing-up procedure itself.'

'How do you mean?'

'When the shift ends, the shift manager prints out the receipts from the credit-card machine and places the money from the cash register into a bag, which he locks in a safe in the staffroom. One barista I spoke to told me that at the end of each day, someone from Kaffikó comes to print out the total takings from the cash register, counts the money in the safe and fills in the cash-up report. Securitas then drives the money to the bank the following day, which is what a lot of companies do, so in that respect everything appears normal. Except for this person who always comes to cash up – that is odd.'

'Could it be they simply don't trust their employees?'

'Maybe,' said Áróra. 'However, most businesses address that problem by installing a camera next to the cash register. It's a lot simpler and cheaper than having someone come in every day to cash up.'

Áróra seemed excited, so Daníel let her go on talking. It was good to see her like this, full of enthusiasm. It occurred to him that maybe she needed more of this in her day-to-day life in Iceland. Challenging work. Excitement.

'This method makes it easy for them to inject large amounts of cash into the business,' Áróra went on. 'Which as far as I can see is exactly what they're doing. None of their competitors take in as much cash. Interestingly, a lot of it is in foreign currency, both euros and dollars.'

'But the money shows up in Kaffikó's accounts, right?'

'Yes, it shows up,' Áróra said. 'And it only looks strange when you compare their cashflow with that of similar businesses. Looking at random samples from the two other coffeehouse chains, I found most of their takings are from card payments rather than cash, very little of which is in foreign currency. In addition, Kaffikó's claim that they get a lot of foreign customers – tourists – doesn't hold up. Their coffeehouses are a long way from all the main tourist attractions and hotels. Their branches are in less prosperous areas of the city, where few tourists go.'

'Amazing!'

'Exactly. And that's why a company, which, to be honest, seemed doomed from the start, on the verge of bankruptcy after its very first year of operation, is now a flourishing business with numerous coffeehouses and record profits. Whether or not this is related to the new investor, it's pretty obvious Kaffikó started laundering money around the time he joined the company.'

'What's the name of this excellent investor of theirs?' Daníel asked, popping a piece of sushi into his mouth.

'Sturla Larsen,' said Áróra, and Daníel was so startled he

nearly choked on his food. 'Too much wasabi?' she asked, but he shook his head, spluttering.

'No,' he said. 'The investor.' He pulled out his phone to call Ari Benz. This would be enough for them to summon Marteinn and Gyða to the station for a serious interrogation. And possibly Sturla, too. The people at Europol would surely be over the moon with this.

'Do you know him?' Áróra asked.

'Yes,' replied Daníel. 'Or rather, I know of him. Some years ago, he was implicated in a major drug-smuggling case, and is now suspected of having connections to foreign criminal gangs.'

'Wow,' Áróra said.

Daníel nodded. The pieces in the Kaffikó puzzle seemed to be coming together.

48

'What exactly did he say about daily fines?' Björn asked once again, pacing back and forth in the living room like a restless animal in far too cramped a cage.

'He said to get in touch with him immediately, otherwise there'd be a daily fine.'

Ísafold had answered the same question over and over again. She had also described the man with yellow hair several times, and with each retelling Björn grew increasingly stressed until she began to wonder whether what Sturla had said about Björn was true; maybe he was a complete coward. In any case, she'd never seen him like this. She was witnessing a completely new side to Björn.

'Did he say his name was Sturla?' Björn asked yet again.

'Yes. He said: "My name's Sturla and I'm not happy."'

'Fuck. Fuck-fuck-fuck!' Björn clenched his fists and stamped his feet.

'Who is this Sturla?' Ísafold asked tentatively.

'He's only one of the biggest drug dealers in Reykjavík,' Björn hissed. 'The man everyone's shit-scared of. They say he killed two guys and got away with it; they also say the guys he killed were lucky. That you're worse off if he catches you alive. Fuck!' Björn's face was red, the veins on his forehead bulged, making it look as if his head was about to explode. 'And you're sure you remembered his name correctly?' he asked Ísafold yet again.

'It's not a name you easily forget,' Ísafold said.

The slap was sharp and the sting on her cheek instant, as if she'd been scalded with hot water.

'None of your lip!' Björn growled.

Ísafold curled up in a corner of the sofa, buried her face in a cushion, anticipating more punches to her sides and back. But when *they didn't come, she lifted her head gingerly and peered in Björn's direction, poised to raise her arms to protect her head. But he continued to pace the floor, muttering to himself, his mind on other things. Ísafold realised it wasn't worth apologising, it would only draw his attention to her again.*

'What are we going to do?' Björn wailed suddenly, startling Ísafold. He didn't usually show much emotion, except occasionally in the days after he'd hit her, when he wanted to work his way back into her good books. She'd never seen him in such a state of agitation.

'Can't we just pay him?' she asked tentatively in her mildest voice.

'Pay him?' Björn yelled. 'How?' He stared at Ísafold with a mixture of contempt and desperation, throwing his hands in the air.

'He looks ruthless but still seems like the kind of guy you can negotiate with. Obviously he wants his money, but he might accept being paid in instalments. I could take on extra shifts and try to take more pills at work. He seemed happy with the two strips I gave him.'

Björn glared at Ísafold, and his expression alone was enough to make the hairs on the back of her neck stand up. Her eyes instinctively measured the distance to the door leading to the hallway. But Björn was blocking her way. She'd need to be more than a little agile to get past him, into the hallway, and from there into the bathroom, where she could lock herself in.

'What did you say you did?' Björn had turned suddenly cold. His desperation giving way to that cruelty she always saw come over him moments before he went crazy. He narrowed his eyes and tilted his head slightly.

'I gave him the two strips I took from work today as part payment of the debt. He seemed happy with them, Björn. He softened, and said "All right, my friend".'

Björn continued to stare at her coldly and Ísafold sat absolutely still, fearing the slightest movement might set him off. Her eyes darted between the doorway and Björn's face, where she anxiously searched for any sign that things might not be as bad as they seemed.

'Do you realise what you've done? Do you understand what you did when you gave him those strips, you stupid idiot?'

Ísafold said nothing, didn't even dare shake her head. She knew he was about to detail to her how badly she'd messed up.

'You confirmed Sturla's suspicions that I'm selling pills. Now I have no way of denying it, I can't claim it was just a few times or a coincidence, or my own medication or something like that. You handed the man two strips, proving to him we've been selling pills, and now he assumes we owe him a shed load of money.'

Ísafold's mind was a blur and she couldn't make sense of this. We? Why did Björn say 'we'? She didn't owe that man anything. And she certainly hadn't been selling pills. She felt her thoughts dance in circles in her head, but she couldn't catch hold of any of them to scrutinise them better. All her energy at that moment was focused on calculating the distance between her and the door. Counting how many steps she needed to take to get past Björn and into the bathroom.

She scarcely had time to think about it, though, before the first punch came, and then she had to tense all her muscles, tighten herself into a small, hard ball, try to protect her face and breasts, gasp for breath between the punches and kicks and hair pulling, until someone banged hard on the door and Grímur's voice out in the hallway shouted something about stopping that damned racket before he called the police.

Björn stormed out to the front door to harangue Grímur, giving Ísafold enough time to escape into the bathroom and lock herself inside.

49

All night long, Felix had been convinced these were his final hours. His back ached so badly from sitting bolt upright tied to a chair, that eventually he gave in and let himself hang forward over the rope wound round his body, allowing his head to droop onto his chest. This stretched his spine a little, and gave him a few moments respite from the pain. He had only a vague idea of who was in the room, as when the boys brought him in, Sturla told them to turn his face to the wall. And here he'd sat for the whole night, awaiting his fate.

They had interrogated him over and over again, demanding he tell them where the bag was, making him describe over and over again how it had simply disappeared from the car when he came out of the convenience store at Hvolsvöllur. Between grillings, he had dozed off to the sound of gun shots and explosions coming from Sturla's computer game, which seemed to merge into a continuous drone that enabled him to close his eyes for a while.

Thoughts of his grandmother kept coming into his head. Grandma, with whom he could always seek refuge. Who had given him a spare key when he was five years old, and told him to come round to her house any time of the day or night if his mum was in one of her bad moods. He had kept the key safe, tied around his neck on a piece of string, for it was his escape from the suffering he endured at the hands of his mother, herself so often the victim of her own unhappiness. Then it was good to go round to Grandma, who always had a smile on her face and something nice to eat in the fridge, a deck of cards at the ready, even though she always lost to him, whether at crazy eights, or, when he was older, at Gin Rummy.

What would Grandma think of him now? He had promised her he'd 'toughen up', as she'd put it, and in fact this was exactly what he'd been doing. It was strange to say but the drug dealers had saved him from becoming an addict. Björn had warned him not to get high on his own supply. Then, after Björn disappeared, or after Sturla had him killed – because surely that's what must have happened – Felix had no choice but to flee the country or go to work for Sturla. And then he became simply too scared to do drugs, as Sturla made it very clear he didn't want any addicts working for him.

Felix flinched when he felt Sturla's clammy hand on the nape of his neck. Neither Sturla nor the boys had beaten or hurt him, however, feeling Sturla's heavy touch was almost worse. Felix's muscles tensed as he braced himself for the pain that didn't come, and the adrenaline flowing through his veins made his heart beat faster and he broke out in a sweat.

'You know I've always had complete trust in you,' said Sturla. He walked calmly in front of Felix, who didn't dare look up, but focused instead on Sturla's long legs ending in slippered feet.

'I know,' whispered Felix. 'And I can be trusted. The thing with the bag was a mega blunder, I get that, but I'm your man, Sturla, totally. You know that. I'm with you.'

Sturla paced round him in a circle, and Felix watched his legs through squinted eyes, tensing his body, waiting for a punch or a kick or a stab, some sort of pain.

'You've been answering back a lot lately,' Sturla said then, and his voice sounded cold. This must be the preamble. Sturla was firing himself up to be able to hit him. 'You feel sorry for my clients,' he went on. 'You give them more time and approve loans, and when I tell you it doesn't pay to be lending money to these people, you give me lip, right?'

'No, Sturla. It's not true, I don't mean to give you lip. I'm just too soft, you know. I feel sorry for those poor people, okay?'

Sturla snorted and paced back and forth in front of Felix for a moment. Then he gave a loud sigh.

'Untie him, lads. I'm bored of this – I need a nap.'

Felix felt someone fiddling behind his back, and then the rope loosened and he was able to take big, deep breaths. The pins and needles in his arms gave way to a burning sensation as the blood flowed back into his hands.

'Take a shower, Felix, my boy,' Sturla said affectionately. 'And go and lie down in the guest room. I have a job for you this afternoon.'

50

After lunch, Ísafold escaped into the TV room, stretched out on the sofa and spread a blanket over her. She would normally have helped Björn's mum, Bryndís, clear the plates away and do the dishes after the Sunday roast, but this time she could barely keep her eyes open. As usual, Bryndís managed to behave as if nothing was wrong, and pretended not to see the black eye Ísafold had been unable to conceal with make-up. Ebbi, on the other hand, had stared at her during lunch, with that look of sympathy she couldn't stand. She knew what he was thinking – she'd heard the lecture often enough, from both him and her sister, Áróra. Neither of them understood why she didn't leave Björn. They didn't understand how she could go on loving him.

As she hovered somewhere between dreams and wakefulness, taking care not to move so the bruises from the beating wouldn't hurt, she heard voices coming from the balcony outside. It was Björn doing all the talking, first in hushed tones, then louder so Ísafold was able to make out the words.

'He'll kill me if I don't pay him!' she heard him say.

Then Ebbi's deep voice took over, calm and deliberate.

'I'm not lending you money to pay off some drug dealer, Björn. It might do you some good to be taught a lesson. You could do with a beating; it might help you put yourself in Ísafold's shoes.'

'Oh, please, don't start on that now.'

'It's terrible to see her like that. Do you think it's normal?'

'Shut your mouth,' Björn said to his brother. 'I know you've always wanted her for yourself, so nothing you say can be taken seriously.' Ísafold heard the balcony door open, followed by footsteps in the living room. Then she heard Björn yell from outside: 'Admit it: you're in love with her!'

Ísafold opened her eyes wide. This didn't bode well. It was never good when Björn got it into his head that some man was in love with her. Then he'd give her a beating. But it was disastrous if he suspected Ebbi, because Ebbi was the person she sought refuge with when things got so bad at home she was forced to leave.

'Pudding!' their mother called out from the kitchen, and Ísafold heard Björn come in from the balcony.

She would pretend to be asleep so she could lie there a bit longer and rest. Björn would never barge in on her here, at his mother's house, so she could safely let her thoughts wander, allow herself gradually to let go until sleep took over.

In her dreams, she was flying, floating in the sky, light as a feather in the breeze, her toes barely brushing the ground to push herself skyward again. This way she was free. No one could catch her, for she needn't even land – she could perch like a bird on a lamppost or in a tree and then take flight from there once more.

51

Áróra felt as if she'd woken up in mid-air. Daníel said he no longer needed her help on the Kaffikó case, and she had no up-coming projects. At least nothing that would stop her from thinking constantly about Ísafold. She went early to The Gym, determined to thoroughly clear her head. A vigorous weightlifting session usually did the trick.

There were three men at The Gym, obviously early risers, all of whom appeared to be working hard to finish their routines, no doubt before going to work. Áróra did her warm-up, skipped and did stretches, preparing her body for the challenge ahead. After the first bench-press lifts, her chest felt lighter, and she was able to take deeper breaths. She moved over to the weight station in the corner and started doing squats. Starting off with a lighter weight she gradually increased the load.

But then, just as the pleasant burning sensation began moving up her thighs, the noise of the other weightlifters around her, the clang of their barbells hitting the racks, their hissing breaths and grunts of exertion, seemed to meld into a single universal pulse that reminded her of a heartbeat.

The tears filled Áróra's eyes and trickled down her cheeks, but she wiped them away and continued her squats with increased zeal. She took on three more lots of weights until, at last, she felt her pain give way to emptiness. She was limp and hollow, like a deflated balloon, encasing nothing.

She strode out of The Gym, trotted across the yard and broke into a sprint when she reached the street, where she headed towards Skólavörðuholt. She felt her feet pounding the tarmac and it occurred to her that it probably wasn't a good idea to run in weightlifting shoes, as they offered very little cushioning. But she batted the thought away. She kept up a brisk pace, slowing every so often before accelerating again, to keep her pulse rate down, to avoid her heart thumping, as she knew where that would lead her thoughts.

The woman at the swimming pool looked at her wearily as she presented her with a worn-looking swimsuit. Áróra nodded and plucked her phone from her tracksuit bottoms in order to pay.

'I need to hire a towel, too,' she said. 'And could I have an orange juice from the cooler as well, please.'

She chugged down the juice on her way to the changing rooms, and could almost feel the cells in her body welcoming the sugar. She could easily have drunk four more on the spot. However, she wasn't there to recharge herself, but to empty herself. Empty her mind, her emotions, until there was nothing left but exhaustion. Then she would feel capable of facing the day. Then she would be able to do the thing she'd been avoiding: call her mum.

The water in the pool cooled her over-heated body and it was pleasant to feel it lapping against her skin. She pushed off and took her first few strokes. She glided through the weightlessness of the water and soon she felt her mind relax, too. She was light and calm, and her strokes became like a kind of meditation. Breathing in, filling her lungs, exhaling, spluttering into the water, kicking to propel herself forward … stretch, kick, stretch, breathe.

Gradually Áróra's strokes fell into a fast and steady rhythm, and then she heard it again, the heartbeat. She stopped at the side of the pool and took a few deep breaths. She sucked in air, swallowed it greedily. She was completely exhausted. Exhausted to the point where she wasn't sure she could heave herself out of the pool. Yet there it was, in her swim strokes, in the pulse of her own circulation, in the water splashing against the sides of the pool. Everywhere, in everything there was a heartbeat.

52

Daníel awoke to a curious noise coming from the garden that sounded remarkably like clucking hens. He rose from his bed, walked over to the window and saw that this was indeed what it was. Clucking. Hens of various colours were strutting all over the lawn, pecking and scratching at the grass that was only just beginning to recover after the winter.

He slipped on a pair of trousers, went out into the garden and stood rubbing his eyes, as if this strange vision might somehow evaporate along with his sleepiness. Just then, Lady Gúgúlú emerged into the garden, her silk dressing gown flapping open to reveal a pair of garish boxer shorts.

'Good morning, Daníel, darling!' she said tossing a handful of seeds to the hens, which immediately scurried over and began to peck.

Daníel shook his head in astonishment. 'Good morning,' he said. 'Why are there hens in my garden?'

'Oh, I couldn't leave my girls behind for a whole week, so I went to pick them up yesterday evening. They're staying in the garden shed.'

Daníel's first reaction was to burst out laughing, until he remembered the shed was where he kept all his tools and garden implements.

'Won't they make a terrible mess?' he asked.

Lady batted away the comment with a flap of her hand. 'Don't exaggerate. They may not be neat freaks, but I'll teach them not to nest on your lawnmower.'

'Will you also clean up after them?' Daníel felt increasingly alarmed. Weren't hen houses smelly? For all he knew these creatures were pooping all over the place. He was fairly fastidious about the garden shed – swept it regularly and liked everything to be in its proper place.

'Naturally, darling,' Lady Gúgúlú replied, as if it were a matter of course.

'You're not exactly a neat freak either,' Daniel said, eliciting laughter.

'Funny you should say that, because he whose name shall not be mentioned said the same thing.'

Daniel wondered whether this remark might be an invitation to broach the subject of Lady's English boyfriend, who had appeared from the past bringing much happiness, but now seemed to have vanished into thin air. He decided to stick to the subject of their feathered friends, who were strutting about and scratching mercilessly at the delicate grass shoots.

'Won't they wreck the lawn?' he asked. Over the years, Daniel had put a lot of effort into keeping the lawn well populated and free of weeds. He usually mowed it once a week, twice if it grew fast, and would pluck out every dandelion that had the temerity to poke its head up anywhere near his lawn.

'No, no, no. Hens are the best thing there is for grass. They aerate the roots and leave behind their droppings, which you can rake into the turf.'

Daniel pulled a face. In other words, the hens would poop everywhere. But Lady wouldn't listen to reason, and the hens were already there, hopefully just for one week.

'Remember this is an apartment block,' said Daniel. 'And we're in the middle of town?'

Lady Gúgúlú snorted. 'Need I remind you of the municipal regulations? It's permitted to keep hens in a built-up area – only cocks are banned. Come to think of it, you might consider banning all cocks from my garage-apartment, except for this one ravishing peacock.' Lady gave a theatrical bow, and Daniel couldn't help but laugh.

'If I'm to ban all cocks from the garage-apartment,' he said, 'maybe you should shave the hair off your chest and your chin. It's unbecoming in a peacock.'

Lady Gúgúlú gave a little cluck, turned on her heel and disappeared inside, while Daníel stood watching the hens busily pecking at the new grass shoots on his lawn.

53

Ísafold was fast asleep when she heard the front door open and a familiar voice call: 'Hello!'

She sat up in bed, rubbed her eyes and tried quickly to arrange her hair. She didn't recall when she'd fallen asleep or why Björn had gone out. The bedroom door opened and in walked Björn holding a big bunch of roses.

'What's this?' Ísafold asked, though she knew perfectly well. It signalled the beginning of a good period.

Björn hung his head and knelt beside her like a repentant sinner. She took the roses from him and breathed in their scent.

'Forgive me,' Björn whispered. 'Forgive me, my love. I don't know what I was thinking. I guess I wasn't thinking at all. I was just stressed out and I lost it.'

He gazed up at her and Ísafold felt the tears trickle down her cheeks. His eyes were full of remorse, the expression on his face sincere, and despite everything, despite the beatings and the cruelty, the ugly things he said to her, Ísafold loved him. She loved him desperately. She set the flowers on the bedside table and spread her arms. He lost himself in her embrace and she wept.

'If you can forgive me I promise I'll never do it again,' he whispered. 'I promise.'

Ísafold felt the pain in her back and sides fade and disappear when Björn rose to his feet, climbed onto the bed, and lay on top of her. His hands caressing her body were gentle and tender, so unlike the hands that had hurt her before, his kisses and his passion were so raw, his remorse so sincere.

'My Björn,' she whispered in his ear and kissed it. 'My Ice-Bear.'

Later, as she lay with her head on his shoulder, his fingers gently caressing the small of her back, a wave of love rippled blissfully *through her. She considered the roses on the bedside table and told herself they heralded a brighter future. They'd get through this. They'd find a way.*

'Will you go and see the counsellor Áróra recommended?' she asked. 'The one who helps men who are violent?'

'Of course,' Björn said. 'I'll do whatever it takes to make things right between us.' He turned on his side, gazed into her eyes and gently stroked her face. 'We just need to deal with Sturla first. You need to bring home as many pills as you can from work.'

Ísafold's warm, naked heart froze.

'I have to be careful not to get caught,' she said, feeling a lump appear in her throat, as painful reality returned. 'I can't just take unlimited amounts.'

The world had done an abrupt volte face. It was as if she'd lost her bearings, time had become fluid and her life was suddenly flowing in the wrong direction. It was the day before yesterday again, Björn was still cold with her, and she was still wondering whether she loved him.

'We'll deal with that when the time comes,' Björn said. 'If you lose this job you can always get another. Right now what matters is that we pay Sturla as much as possible of this so-called debt.'

54

The look on the face of the young boy serving at the hotdog stand outside the swimming baths verged on concern, as he handed Áróra her fourth hotdog with all the trimmings.

'You must be very hungry,' he said.

Áróra nodded. 'I practically did a triathlon this morning,' she replied, taking the hotdog and chocolate milk from him. 'Plus I skipped breakfast, so my glycogen levels need topping up.'

The lad continued to look at her uneasily. 'The record here is three,' he said. 'But that's when the stand is outside the building-supply store, Húsasmiðja, as tradesmen are ravenous by lunchtime. The biggest guys can eat three, and maybe a chocolate bar afterwards.'

Áróra was halfway through the hotdog and considering ordering a fifth just to amuse the lad, but that would be to waste food. She couldn't eat any more and threw the remaining half into the rubbish bin.

'I've broken your record with three and a half, in any case,' she said to the lad, before heading back to The Gym, where she'd left her car.

She felt heavy now, her stomach full and her muscles exhausted. And she didn't like having to put her sweaty training clothes back on after her swim. Catching a whiff of cold sweat on herself, she planned her schedule for the day. A schedule she could live by. She would go home, take a shower, get dressed and read everything she could about Sturla Larsen, Kaffikó's mysterious investor who Daníel said had connections to criminal gangs.

Only when she was focused on some project, a project that really interested her did her mood lighten. If physical exercise didn't do the trick, then the next best medicine was work. Although Daníel had told her he didn't need any more information, Áróra still intended to investigate this guy. Agla would at least be happy to have a medium-sized money-laundering case to work on. It was clear as day that Kaffikó was laundering money, the only question was, where did the money come from?

Áróra was slightly out of breath when she arrived at her car, parked outside The Gym. There'd been a strong headwind most of the way along Snorrabraut and with her legs half numb from the morning's exertions she'd found walking difficult. Yet despite the breathlessness and the pulsing in her ears, despite thinking about Ísafold and her missing heart, she was no longer hurting. No longer wounded to the quick, because she had a project. Maybe her mother was right when she called her a workaholic. It was certainly true that she used work as a way of avoiding difficult emotions.

It occurred to her briefly to call her mother, get it over with. Tell her she'd heard about Ísafold's body being found with the heart missing. But she pushed the idea aside. There was no point in stirring things up with her mum, before any new information emerged regarding Ísafold's death. If indeed any did.

55

Marteinn couldn't conceal the rage simmering inside him. He wore a morose expression as he sat at the table in the interview room, legs apart, one foot set back and to the side of his chair, as if he were poised to take off the instant the starting gun sounded.

'What's this really about?' he asked, the instant Daníel walked in.

Daníel smiled genially, taking his time to arrange his folder, papers and pen on the table in front of him. 'Would you like a coffee or some other refreshment?' he asked politely. 'We have a decent coffee machine up on the top floor, though I can't promise the quality will measure up to what you're used to.'

Marteinn shook his head. 'No, thanks. I'd just like to know why you've called me in here for an interview.'

'Like I said before, we're looking into a couple of cases which it seems were incorrectly processed in the system, and there are a few loose ends we want to tie up.' Marteinn opened his mouth to speak, but Daníel raised his finger in the air. 'I'd like to begin by explaining to you how this whole process works. This room we're in is equipped with recording devices and cameras – there and there.' He pointed to the cameras. 'And my colleagues involved in the investigation can follow this conversation in real time on their own computers, or listen to it later in the system.'

Marteinn shot a glance at the cameras, and Daníel could see from the man's expression that he'd achieved the intended effect with his preamble. Marteinn was now imagining officers all over the station hanging on their every word, and it clearly made him uneasy. The truth was, however, that probably no one was listening, except maybe Ari Benz.

'What is this about, exactly?' Marteinn asked again, and when

Daníel prevaricated, giving him the same spiel about past cases and tying up loose ends, Marteinn cut in. 'I don't understand what the problem is. Our property was vandalised and we couldn't be bothered to follow it up. End of story, okay?'

'Hm.' Daníel leaned back in his chair and contemplated Marteinn for a few moments.

Marteinn held his gaze then raised his hands in the air questioningly. 'What's going on?'

'Well,' said Daníel, sitting up straight again and leafing through the folder as if to refresh his memory. 'We're wondering why you reported the damage to your vehicle and house, but not the killing of your dog.'

Marteinn gaped at him in astonishment, then quickly recovered himself. 'We don't know for sure that someone killed our dog; it could have been an accident.'

'I gather the animal's throat was cut,' Daníel said.

Marteinn snorted. 'Who told you that?' Daníel didn't reply, but kept looking at Marteinn, who went on. 'Maybe he got caught up in some barbed wire.'

'Is there barbed wire in your garden?'

'No, but you know what I mean. Dogs will be dogs, and this one was quite lively.'

'I see.' Daníel leafed through the folder again, pulled out the picture of Marteinn and Gyða with Sturla Larsen and placed it on the table in front of Marteinn. 'What we're wondering,' he said, 'is whether the damage to your coffeehouse and your home, and the subsequent killing of your dog, might be linked to Sturla.'

Now Marteinn was visibly unsettled. He tugged at the neck of his shirt to loosen the collar.

'Sturla?' he echoed.

'Yes.' Daníel paused then added: 'For the recording: we're talking about a certain Sturla Larsen, whose name has been linked to various cases the police have investigated.'

'If you're drawing conclusions from a photograph taken at a celebration marking the opening of a coffeehouse, I can tell you I don't remember every person I invited to all these parties. We invite all sorts of people, and some of them bring guests.'

Daníel raised his eyebrows questioningly. 'You mean you don't remember Sturla? Your main investor? No, what am I saying: your only investor?'

'Are you behind this trouble with the tax people?' Marteinn now raised his voice. 'Is this some kind of conspiracy to try to tarnish our reputation and put pressure on the company?'

Daníel adopted an air of innocent bewilderment. 'Re-ally.' He drew out the word. 'So, the Directorate of Tax Investigations is looking into your company?'

Marteinn clenched his jaw, making the muscles ripple beneath his skin. 'They've asked for some data they call random samples. Just like you, who claim to be re-examining past cases when in fact you're investigating something completely different.' He stared defiantly at Daníel, who still feigned a look of surprise. Then Marteinn murmured: 'I just wonder whether it's a coincidence that these public institutions have decided to persecute my company, or whether you're all in it together.'

'It's certainly an interesting theory and, if necessary, we can ask the Directorate of Tax Investigations to share that data with us,' Daníel said, and watched as Marteinn slowly shrank back in his seat. He then drew both of his feet under his chair and folded his arms. 'But let's go back to acts of vandalism,' Daníel resumed. 'And to Sturla. Your investor. The term they sometimes use in English to describe people who put money into an ailing business in exchange for little or no return is "angel investors". But Marteinn, you and I both know that Sturla Larsen is no angel.'

'No comment,' Marteinn said, staring intently at the table.

'I'm going to be completely frank with you Marteinn,' Daníel said, slamming the folder shut in front of him. 'I'm going to tell you what I'm thinking. I'm wondering whether, far from being an angel who came to save your business, Sturla was the exact opposite. A devil who has taken over your company and is forcing you to launder his ill-gotten gains – because, yes, Sturla Larsen's links to the drug trade and possible links to international criminal gangs are well known. I'm wondering whether Sturla has resorted to threats and acts of vandalism to drive home the fact that you have no choice but to do what he says.'

Marteinn sprang to his feet and paced back and forth across the room. The sleeves of his blue shirt, no doubt freshly ironed that morning, were now crumpled, and a dark-blue sweat stain was spreading across his back. 'Where the hell did you get that idea from?' he shouted. He crossed the room two more times before slumping back in his chair angrily. 'I want a lawyer,' he said.

Daníel smiled genially again. 'Of course,' he said. 'Let's take a break.'

56

Helena hardly dared glance over at Vala, who was sitting on the far side of the open-plan office, conscientiously trawling through four-year-old logs from the Suðurnes police. Every time Helena looked at her, Vala seemed to sense it and would look up with that half-smile she'd been wearing since their conversation the previous day. The conversation had started awkwardly, and ended, to put it mildly, embarrassingly. So embarrassingly that Helena was still unsure how to behave.

Vala had begun by asking Helena if she was single, and Helena had said yes, because she could hardly admit to the rookie cop that Sirra and Bisi's marriage was fake, and that the three of them were breaching immigration rules. However, this confirmation had emboldened Vala, who promptly asked her out on a date. Helena had declined, saying it wasn't an option while Vala was shadowing her, to which Vala had retorted: 'But what about when I'm no longer in training? I finish my placement in three weeks.'

Taken aback that her refusal hadn't been enough, Helena murmured words to the effect that it might be better to see how things stood when the time came. Vala seemed to regard this as a promise of a future a date, rather than Helena trying to wriggle out of the offer, because since then she'd been giving her meaningful smiles and fluttering her long eyelashes alluringly whenever their gazes crossed. Helena could tell it would be tricky to disentangle herself. Vala was undeniably attractive, and there was a time when Helena would have jumped at the offer, but it was as if Sirra had erased all other women from her mind and her heart.

Helena was busy logging yesterday's notes on the police database when Vala called out: 'Hey, look at this.'

Helena got to her feet, and went over to Vala, only this time, instead of that knowing half-smile, the other woman was fully focused on the computer screen in front of her. 'Here it's noted in their log that police monitoring traffic on Reykjanesbraut stopped a driver who tested positive when breathalysed. It seems he was on his way to the airport, and it says here that after accompanying him to have a blood test they drove him to the terminal. However, because they didn't fine him, his ID number wasn't entered into the system.'

'I expect they get several cases like that every week,' Helena said, disappointed. For all Vala's excitement, what she'd discovered didn't seem very significant.

'It's the closing observations that are interesting, though,' Vala went on. 'It says here the driver was far too early for the morning flight to London he intended to take, and would have had to wait several hours in the terminal, but when asked about this he said he wanted to be on time.'

'Strange observation,' Helena said. 'Clearly not much of interest happened on their shift.'

'Isn't it worth following up?' asked Vala. 'Here are the names of the officers in question,' she added, pointing at the screen. Helena memorised the names, went back to her desk and looked up the Suðurnes police. One of the officers was clearly still working there so she dialled the number for the Suðurnes police station.

57

Jóhann, a police officer on the Suðurnes peninsula, didn't have to think too hard to recall the incident described in the log, when nearly four years ago he and his colleague María stopped a driver on Reykjanesbraut.

'Yes, I remember it well. The guy was one of the strangest individuals I've ever met. He was a bit drunk, as I recall, tested positive on the breathalyser, so we took him to the health centre in Keflavík for a blood test. His alcohol levels weren't high enough for us to slap a fine on him, so we dropped him off at the airport, parked his car for him, and my colleague María gave him a brief lecture on the evils of drink-driving.'

'I see,' said Helena. 'But you didn't note down his name?'

'No. Because we didn't fine him. And I doubt we entered the incident on the database, only in the diary log. The health centre might have a record of his ID number, because of the blood test, if you really need to find it.' Jóhann's voice had a questioning tone, but Helena didn't share any further information. She just looked at Vala, who was listening to the phone call and nodding while she took notes.

'Okay. And you're sure you don't remember the guy's name?'

'No. What is it you're looking into?'

'We're just going over data relating to an old case, double-checking a few things. Can you at least describe the man, seeing as how you remember the incident so well.'

'Yes. I certainly can. He was extremely nervous – mind you, a lot of people are before they fly, and being flagged down by the police didn't help. But then he came out with this legendary remark: "Well, I just want to be on time." Which was hilarious, you see, because the guy would have arrived six hours early at the airport. It became a running joke at the station whenever someone got stressed about being late: "Well, I just want to be on time."' Jóhann laughed out loud, but when Helena barely gave a chuckle, his laughter died out. 'You had to be there to see the funny side. In any case, we always had hysterics whenever anyone mentioned the guy.'

'What was so strange about him, exactly?'

'It was his voice, and then the wig.' Helena felt her body warm up as her heart began to race in her chest.

'Did you say he wore a wig?'

'Yes, a really bad wig that didn't suit him at all because he had such pale skin.'

'Do you remember what car he drove?'

'Noooo,' Jóhann said, drawing out the last word. 'Some old rust bucket – an estate, as I recall.'

'Thanks. You've been incredibly helpful,' Helena said, before hanging up. Then she looked at Vala and said: 'The Icelandic Civil Aviation Administration. We need to get hold of the passenger lists from that day. And, if you can, find out whether the car park keeps a vehicle record. Then there's the health centre at Keflavík. We'll need a warrant to access their database.'

Vala got on the phone instantly, and Helena went back to her desk. She was preparing her request for the warrant, when her phone rang. It was Officer Jóhann again.

'Hey, it so happens I keep all my old notebooks stacked in my locker here, and I've managed to find the one from the night we stopped that strange guy. And guess what? I wrote down his number plate!'

Helena wanted to howl with joy, but only permitted herself an exultant 'Yessssss!' as she opened the vehicle-registration database on her computer.

58

Felix didn't dare to stay under the hot shower as long as he'd have liked. He was half expecting someone to burst into the bathroom at any moment, jump on him, tie him up and beat him, or possibly do something worse. After showering, he wrapped himself in a towel, rolled his clothes into a bundle under his arm, then peered out into the corridor. There was no one about and the house was quiet. The bangs and rumbling emanating from the computer game downstairs had ceased, and he couldn't hear any voices. Maybe this wasn't a trick or ruse after all. Maybe he could actually lie down and have a rest.

He tiptoed along the hallway and slipped noiselessly into the guest room. It was spacious, without any wardrobes or alcoves where someone might hide, so Felix closed the door behind him and turned the small button lock. He knew better than anyone this type of lock was pretty feeble and could be opened with a table knife. He'd learned that when he was twelve. Putting down his clothes and towel, he took hold of the chest of drawers over by the bed, and carried it across the room, then carefully slid it in front of the door as noiselessly as possible. It was no obstacle for a strong man but might buy him some time. He could maybe jump out of the window, although it looked a bit high; or at least brace himself to respond to a beating. He perched on the edge of the bed, but his aching back demanded he lie down and within seconds he was fast asleep.

The light had changed when he awoke to the sound of the doorbell. It seemed like he'd been asleep for a long time, but when he checked the clock on his phone, he saw that it wasn't even midday. He was far from refreshed, his head felt dull and heavy, and whenever he moved, every cell in his body cried out in pain. Was this what the boys called being put in the torture chair? Being forced to sit still all night long, while Sturla played a computer game behind you? In any case, his body felt like it had taken a beating after all.

His mind instantly went into overdrive as he recalled the convenience store at Hvolsvöllur and those fateful few minutes. He was positive he had locked the car before entering the store. Last night when he was on the chair, he'd told Sturla and the guys that he would never have left the bag unattended in the car without locking it. Not only that, but he'd scarcely taken his eyes off the car when he was inside the store. For a few seconds at most – not long enough for someone to pick the lock. And that was the other mystery. There were no signs anyone had tampered with the car. He had puzzled endlessly over whether it was even possible to pick the lock on such a car. The electronic locking systems were completely different on these new models.

Felix sat up in bed and placed his feet cautiously on the floor, as though afraid the floorboards might creak. This was a stone house, however, and he made no sound as he stood up and tiptoed over to the adjoining bathroom. It was so small there was barely room for a toilet and the tiniest basin he'd ever seen. Still, he slipped inside, closing the door behind him, as he couldn't urinate with his back to an open door. He tried to aim the stream at the edge of the bowl to make less noise, and considered whether or not to flush. If he did, it would be a sure sign to anyone in the house who was awake that he was up and about, and they might grab him again and put him back in the chair. He couldn't imagine what punishment Sturla might deem appropriate for someone who lost a whole bag of money, but it had to be something worse than a night in the torture chair.

He got dressed, slicked his hair down with water as best he could, then gently inched the chest of drawers away from the door, opened it and crept out of the room. The hallway was empty except for the sound of faint music that reached him from below, and he slowly made his way down the stairs.

There was no one in the living room, but the radio was on. In the kitchen Sturla and two of his boys sat at the table, slicing open bundles of banknotes. They were wrapped in black plastic, the same as the ones in the bag Felix had lost. They opened one package after another and stacked the notes in neat piles in the middle of the table, then threw the plastic on the floor.

'Felix, my man!' Sturla declared, beaming.

Felix forced a smile as he walked over to the table and gazed at the pile of money. The bundles of notes seemed to expand once they were liberated from the vacuum-sealed plastic. 'The operation is in full swing here,' Sturla said, eyeing the two boys: 'Time for lunch, lads. Bacon sandwiches all round, please.'

While the two boys vacated the kitchen, Sturla motioned for Felix to sit down on the chair next to him. Then he grabbed a backpack from the floor and began filling it with the banknotes from the piles on the table.

'Euros, Felix, my man, dollars and pounds. Your job is to distribute them evenly between locations.'

'Huh?' Felix felt his head start to swim. He was utterly confused. 'You're not sending me off with money again, are you?'

Sturla laughed, turned to him and clasped his shoulder firmly. 'There's no one more trustworthy and loyal than somebody who owes you money. And you, Felix my man, owe me a whole bag full of money. I know you won't make the same mistake twice, and that now you've well and truly learned not to take your eyes off the bag. Which is why I'm promoting you to cashier.'

He tossed the backpack into Felix's lap, squeezed his shoulder in a friendly manner and smiled. And then Felix knew for sure that the sneaking suspicion he had when he first saw the piles of banknotes on the table was true. As he sat and looked straight into Sturla's eyes, any doubts he'd had evaporated. It was Sturla himself who'd arranged for the bag of money to be stolen from him outside the convenience store in Hvolsvöllur.

59

Sturla Larsen didn't cut much of a figure, Áróra thought. His bleached hair had turned a yellowish colour, except for the dark roots that were quite noticeable. He was thin, his long legs splayed in front of him as he sat on a deep sofa in the living room. Áróra had spent the day reading everything she could find about him, and had concluded he was some sort of Teflon-man; apart from an old drug-smuggling conviction, nothing stuck to him officially, although Daníel maintained his name had been linked to numerous drugs cases. And now here she was, standing in the living room of his house in the Grafarholt suburb of Reykjavík, which was decorated like a hotel lobby, with huge marble floor tiles and mirror-lined walls. On an enormous shelving unit stood two gigantic loudspeakers that wouldn't have looked out of place in a small nightclub. Otherwise, the shelves groaned under the weight of vodka bottles of varying brands. Sturla was in the middle of playing a computer game, and had his dragon avatar lob a few more bombs at his enemies before pressing the pause button and looking up at Áróra.

'Who did you say you were?' he asked, and one of the young men, whose sole function seemed to be to watch Sturla play computer games, rose to his feet and positioned himself behind his boss, like a tracksuited bodyguard.

The youth who had reluctantly let Áróra into the house, took up his position behind her, but when she moved further into the room and stood with her back against the wall next to the television, he was forced to stand beside her. That was better. She always felt uncomfortable standing with her back to people she didn't trust. And the atmosphere in the room didn't inspire trust. All she could see on the table were fizzy drinks cans and sweet wrappers, however, this group of men looked as if they might have a sizeable weapons cache somewhere.

'My name is Áróra,' she said. 'I work for the Property Tax Evaluation Department, due to some changes in the way we calculate property tax, we're measuring a number of properties.' She whipped out the laser pen she'd bought thirty minutes earlier at a DIY store and switched it on. The beam danced about the room until she gained control of it, and projected it onto the wall behind Sturla, turning in a half-circle until it was projecting onto the opposite wall.

Sturla watched her in amazement but then snapped his fingers. The tracksuited man leapt to attention, grabbed a tablet off one of the shelves, typed something into it and handed it to Sturla, who swiped his finger across the screen a few times then shook his head.

'I can't find you on the Property Tax Evaluation Department's website,' he said. 'There's no Áróra on the staff list there.'

'I'm not an employee, I'm a contractor, a freelance—'

Sturla cut her off: 'Do you have ID?' he asked.

Áróra felt in her pocket for her wallet and pulled out her tattered driver's licence.

Sturla took it and inspected it. 'This is just a driver's licence,' he said.

'Yes, didn't you want to see some ID?'

'I'd like to see some ID that proves you work for the Property Tax Evaluation Department,' he said.

'Oh, I see. We don't have anything like that,' she said then. 'Didn't you receive the letter they sent? They always send a letter in advance notifying that a property is due to be measured, along with the name of the subcontractor who will carry out the work. My name should be on that letter, if you can find—'

'I didn't receive any letter.' Sturla gazed at her intently, and Áróra realised the game was up. She'd hoped to be able to wander round the house, pretending to be measuring something with her laser, while attempting to discover more about this mysterious man. But it was obvious he was more suspicious than most. 'You can come back when you have the proper identification, or some other documentation proving you have the right to be here.' He jerked his head and the two men instantly grabbed Áróra by the arms, practically dragging her in the direction of the front door.

She struggled, hissing that she could walk by herself, and they released their grip, but stayed on her heels. One of them halted at the front door while the tracksuited one followed her all the way out to the driveway and onto the street, as if he wanted to make absolutely certain she intended to leave.

'Relax,' Áróra said to the man, who wouldn't give up and accompanied her all the way out to her car.

'You relax,' he retorted thickly.

She climbed in and drove off, watching in her rear-view mirror as the man went back inside. She drove down the street, then turned up the next one and came back, parking in a spot where she could keep an eye on Sturla's house.

60

Ísafold had felt awful at work all day. She was sweating, had a headache, and every time she opened the door to a resident's apartment her heart pounded so fast she could feel the veins in her temples expand and contract with a whoosh.

Ísafold forced a smile as she entered Vigdís's living room. She was a delicate woman who suffered from the shakes but somehow seemed full of energy. The instant she saw Ísafold, she came alive, rose from her chair and went to rummage in the kitchen cupboards for a snack to offer her.

'Would you like some kleinur, my dear?' There was something about the way the old woman said this, or maybe it was the look of joy on her face when Ísafold arrived, that made her well up. Here was this woman offering her treats, unaware that Ísafold intended to steal from her.

She nodded, perched on a chair and took one of the kleinur from the tin Vigdís held out to her.

'My son is a keen baker. He always brings me some nice treat when he visits,' she said. 'Home-baked pastries are so much nicer than that stuff they sell at the supermarket.'

'It's true,' Ísafold said, and smiled again. 'You need help with your medication, don't you?' she said then.

The old lady nodded, reaching for another tin, one for ginger biscuits. 'This is my pill box,' she said. 'They all come in rolls now, but the print is so small I can't read the dates, so I don't know which is the morning dose and which the evening.'

Ísafold opened the tin and discovered, to her dismay, that it contained only the medication roll. She took the list of drugs and read through it. Blood pressure pills and anti-rheumatics; and then she saw it: Tramadol 'when needed'.

'I see you also have painkillers. Where do you keep them?' she asked.

Vigdís shook her head. 'I don't need any right now. They're in the bathroom because I sometimes take one at night, if the pain keeps me awake. Only occasionally, though.'

Ísafold smiled and opened the dosage blisters for the old lady. She dutifully took her pills, before launching into a long story about how much fun dances were in the old days. Ísafold was momentarily drawn into Vigdís's account as she munched on a kleinur, then another, between sips from a small glass of milk. She imagined Vigdís in an elegantly tailored silk dress, wearing a pearl necklace and fur coat, walking home after the ball at Iðnó Theatre with her friend, who was so drunk she fell into Tjörnin Pond. Vigdís's laughter as she recalled the scene was so infectious that for a moment Ísafold forgot about her own life, and a light, airy feeling came over her, which she supposed must be joy. But then reality came crashing down on her once more as she remembered Björn and the pills she was supposed to steal, and she felt her stomach tighten and bile rise up her throat.

'Thank you for the refreshments,' she said, and went to put her glass in the sink. 'May I use your bathroom before I go? It's such a long way to run down to the staff toilets.'

'Of course, my dear,' said Vigdís, and Ísafold hurried into the bathroom.

Inside, she carefully opened the cupboard in search of the Tramadol, and cursed her luck when she found only one blister strip in the packet. What if Vigdís awoke in the night in pain and needed her pills? She stood holding the strip and going over in her mind everything Björn had said about doctors writing endless prescriptions for elderly people, how they only had to call to get more drugs. And that Sturla would kill him if he didn't pay off his debt in good time.

Ísafold flushed the toilet, turned on the tap and let it run for a while. Then she slipped the strip into her pocket.

61

A strong northerly breeze had blown up when Felix came out of the second coffeehouse, making him wish his old Volvo had a heated steering wheel like the luxury car he'd driven east to Seyðisfjörður. Not that he couldn't afford a better car on the salary Sturla paid him, but he was saving up every penny he could because he wanted to buy his own apartment. He didn't intend to do what some of the lads did who worked for Sturla: wallow in luxury, adorn themselves with gold chains and expensive watches, drive round in fancy cars and be unable to pay their bills. But now his dream of becoming his own man, beholden to no one, was most likely over. He had the impression the backpack on the seat next to him was screaming at him. Screaming that he was an idiot. He could have kicked himself for walking so easily into Sturla's trap. He should have known this was how Sturla operated. If people didn't end up owing him money through their own foolishness, he simply fabricated a debt. And it made no difference that Sturla probably knew Felix realised it was all a sham. If Sturla said he owed him, then that was that. Felix didn't dare contradict him.

He pulled up outside the third coffeehouse, on Skipholt, and went inside. The café was empty apart from the barista, who stood polishing the coffee machine.

'I'm here to cash up,' he said, and the girl nodded.

'They told me they'd be sending someone new from the company. Have you worked for Kaffikó for long?'

Felix smiled and shook his head. 'No, not really. A few months, maybe.' Sturla had told him how to respond, should anyone ask. He was to give vague, woolly answers while pretending he worked for Kaffikó.

'Would you like anything? A coffee, a sandwich or something else?'

Felix shook his head and went over to the cash register. He logged in using the password Sturla had given him, which provided access to the safes and cash registers in all the coffeehouses, and changed on the first of every month. He pulled the scrap of paper from his pocket and entered the amounts written on it: 2,300 euros, 960 pounds, 400 dollars. The figures were roughly the same for each café – euros mostly, dollars least. Then he printed out the end-of-day total and tore it off the till roll.

'Okay,' he said. 'Where's the safe?'

Felix noticed a look of dismay on the girl's face as she pointed him towards the back room. No doubt she'd been hoping for a bit of chit-chat. Clearly, there wasn't a lot for her to do here.

The safe was on the floor in a corner of the back room. Felix opened it with the combination and pulled out a blue cash bag. The contents were rather meagre. A few thousand kronur notes, a handful of loose change and then a bunch of credit-card receipts. Icelanders paid almost exclusively by card nowadays, but judging from the number of receipts, this coffeehouse didn't take many card payments either. Felix opened the backpack and drew out the banknotes. The euros and pounds were simple as they came in bundles of a thousand, then he counted out the loose dollars. He placed them in the cash bag along with the receipts, zipped it shut, put a plastic security seal on it and locked it inside the safe again. Sturla had explained the procedure to him in great detail, insisting that each step needed to be carried out to the letter – but it wasn't exactly rocket science. He'd get faster at it the more practice he got. It might not be exciting work, but it was a thousand times better than having to squeeze pennies out of poor addicts, or beat people up.

He waved goodbye to the girl as he walked back past the counter, and no sooner had he stepped outside onto the pavement than he sensed it. The hairs on the back of his neck stood up and his heart starting pounding fast. Someone was watching him. He glanced about, and his eye alighted on a white electric car across the street. Hadn't he seen it before? Outside the last café? The idea that he was being followed filled him with dread, and he felt a shiver run down his spine. Who could it be? Was it the police? Or someone planning to steal the money from him? Could it be someone working for Sturla, sent to make sure he did everything properly? He could understand why Sturla might do that; after all, he was carrying a substantial amount of money in his backpack when he started the run, and even though Sturla had staged the theft at Hvolsvöllur, Félix had allowed the bag to be stolen, which showed he probably wasn't a hundred percent reliable.

He rushed over to his car and turned on the engine. He had to be sure before he did anything rash. He drove off, cruised slowly along Skipholt then made an abrupt left turn onto Brautarholt, without paying attention to whether he was driving against the traffic or not. Then he stepped on the accelerator, turned down Nóatún, speeding up again until he reached Laugavegur, where he raced in the direction of Suðurlandsbraut. Glancing in his rear-view mirror, he saw to his horror that the white car was behind him, several car lengths back, but still on his tail. It must have jumped a red light to avoid losing him. Félix knew for sure now that he was being followed. Once more, he felt his heart hammer in his chest, and he concentrated on taking slow, deep belly breaths to try to regain control of his emotions.

He went through all the options in his head. If this was the police, he would have to abort his rounds and try somehow to hide the backpack, which still contained the money for several coffeehouses. A good idea might be to drive up to Öskjuhlíð, pull over and make a dash for the wooded area. There was a chance he could lose them there, maybe even conceal the backpack somewhere in the undergrowth.

If, on the other hand, this was someone planning to try to rob him, he should head straight to the nearest coffeehouse, stash the backpack in the safe and call Sturla, who could send his boys to rough up whoever was following him. The problem was, how could he know whether it was the police or thieves? While he was considering this, the third possibility occurred to him again. If Sturla had sent someone to keep an eye on him, he needed to show them he knew he was being tailed and also that it was pissing him off.

He'd reached Grensásvegur and from there he turned into Ármúli, then took a sharp left up the side street, where he slowed down to see if the car was still following him. It was, and Felix pulled up close to the kerb and put on his warning lights, as if the car had broken down. He slipped on the backpack as he stepped out, and walked to the front of the car, opened the bonnet, and leaned over the engine. Whoever was following him would be forced to slow down and drive on by. It would be too obvious if they simply pulled up behind him.

This gave Felix a brief opportunity, which he seized. As the white car rolled slowly past, he leapt out in front of it and raised his hands, as though flagging it down for assistance. To his astonishment, the driver was a woman, and she was alone. She lowered her window halfway, and he walked up to the driver's door.

'You wouldn't have a jack, would you?' he said, before realising that an open bonnet and a jack didn't necessarily go together, so he hurriedly added: 'I think my water tank has a crack in it and I need to take a look underneath. If you can lend me a jack, it'll only take two minutes.'

The woman eyed him warily and seemed disinclined to open the car door, so Felix thrust one arm through the window, grabbed her by the neck and squeezed her throat as hard as he could.

'Unlock the car,' he hissed. 'Now!'

She tried to wriggle free then did what he would have done in her place, pressed the button to raise the window. But Felix was prepared. He grabbed the rim of the window with his free hand and tugged it so hard it broke, then, using the same hand, reached inside and unlocked the door. Felix released his grip on the woman, who spluttered and gasped for breath, then swiftly installed himself on the back seat, whipped out a piece of cord he kept in his pocket for such occasions and looped it deftly about her neck and pulled it tight.

The woman gave up any attempt to struggle when she felt the cord tighten round her throat. She sat upright and immobile, hands raised in a sign of submission. He studied her in the rear-view mirror. Her blonde hair fell over her face, and she had a look of fear in her eyes, though he thought he also glimpsed a flash of defiance.

'Drive,' he said.

62

Time seemed to have distorted when the man pulled the cord tight about her neck, so that Áróra had the impression she'd been driving for ages, though probably only a few minutes had passed. The man had ordered her to drive, but hadn't specified where. She had gone round the block a few times then driven up Suðurlandsbraut, and was now on Miklabraut, heading downtown.

'What do you want?' Áróra asked, her question ending in a splutter when he yanked on the cord – apparently an automatic response to her speaking. He was clearly jumpy.

'Who sent you?' he hissed.

Áróra had no idea what he was talking about and ignored the question. Her eyes cast about desperately for an escape, which was difficult because she could hardly move her head. The traffic around Kringlan was heavy, and Miklabraut looked congested as they approached the city centre.

'I'm going to take a right,' she said, putting on her indicator to turn onto Kringlumýrabraut.

He grunted his approval behind her. This was a good decision. One lane was fairly clear and in the other only an occasional car trundled towards the seafront. She slowed the car down until it crept forward.

'What are you doing?' the young man hissed. 'Why are we going so slowly?'

She pointed to her neck, and he loosened the cord slightly. That was enough to reignite the anger that had flared in Áróra when he forced his way into her car. She stepped on the accelerator and the car sped forward; at the same time she slid her hand under the cord, clasped hold of it and slammed on the brakes, quickly jerking the steering wheel to the right, then taking her foot off the brake before slamming it down again.

The man was thrown off balance, enabling Áróra to free herself enough to turn partially in her seat. She rammed her fist into his face, still clutching the cord with her left hand and praying it wouldn't cut into her throat.

The blow to the man's face was sufficiently heavy and sudden to make him release his grip, and Áróra was able to free herself. She tore the cord from about her neck, shot out of the car and yanked open the back door, where the man was rubbing his nose, which was gushing blood. She had the advantage now, as she stood over him and he was wedged in the back seat. She leaned down to grab hold of him, but as she did so he managed to land a hefty blow on her forehead, and for a split second everything went black. But this actually helped, as the pain intensified the flood of adrenaline filling her body and any sympathy she might have had for the guy evaporated. She didn't care if she hurt him. She didn't care if she hurt him badly.

She grabbed him by the hair and yanked his head forward, ramming her knee as hard as she could into his face. The blow was so powerful she lost her grip on his hair but grabbed his sweatshirt instead and proceeded to drag him out of the car. He seemed dazed and half slumped onto the street. She rolled him with kicks and blows onto a traffic island, where he lay on his side curled up in a ball, his sweatshirt hiked up, exposing his white back with a tattooed image of a roaring tiger.

Áróra climbed into her car, and drove off at speed. In the rear-view mirror she saw the man struggle to his knees before falling back on his side, where he lay immobile. She pounded on the steering wheel, then screamed a few times to burn off some of the adrenaline, excitement and fear, and to loosen her vocal cords and throat, which stung like hell.

63

'Europol thanks us for the information and asks if we could hold off while they complete their end of the investigation,' Ari Benz said.

Daníel sighed. This was the perfect example of a so-called 'collaborative project'. Europol asked for information but gave none in return.

Ari Benz gazed at him sympathetically. 'I realise how frustrating this is, and if you want I can discuss it with the commissioner, although the custom is that we hold off when asked to do so by outside agencies.'

'Yes, I know.' Daníel sat with his face in his hands and rubbed his forehead. This was indeed frustrating. He had backed Marteinn into a corner and he was starting to feel the pressure. From there it might only be a matter of time before he started spilling the beans.

'They say things are at a sensitive stage.'

'I see.'

'And then there's one ... other matter.' Ari Benz seemed embarrassed. 'They've asked you to keep your girlfriend in check. Somehow they've found out that she's also poking around in Kaffikó's affairs.'

Daníel groaned. He wasn't going to make any excuses or explain about this; arguably, he shouldn't have mentioned the case to Áróra, and doing so could be regarded as breach of confidentiality. Equally, there was a strong tradition within the police to use outside advisers when working on cases that required specialist knowledge, as Ari himself was well aware. He got to his feet and took his leave.

As he strolled from the National Police Commissioner's

Office to the station, Daníel reflected about how he might approach this with Áróra. She'd become so excited about the case, and had been a great help, so he mustn't come across as ungrateful after all her hard work.

Back at the station, Marteinn sat waiting in the interview room, now accompanied by his lawyer, who sat tapping his pen on the table, clearly prepared to confront any difficult questions.

'Hello,' Daníel said, extending his arm and shaking the lawyer's hand vigorously. 'I apologise for having called you out on this occasion. Upon closer consideration, we have no more questions to put to Marteinn. We don't intend to investigate the matter further; however, it's for the commissioner to decide whether there are grounds to refer Kaffikó to the economic-crime unit.'

The lawyer seemed relieved and returned his pen to his pocket, but the expression on Marteinn's face suggested he'd prefer a murder charge to an investigation into Kaffikó's finances.

'Very well,' the lawyer said, rising to his feet. 'Let's go, Marteinn.'

'Yes. Thank you for coming to talk to us and apologies for the inconvenience,' Daníel said, and left the room.

64

Ísafold was late leaving work. The manager had marched over just as she was getting ready to go home and asked her to come downstairs to help accompany the residents back to their apartments after bingo, as the girl on the evening shift was running late. Ísafold had given an almost hysterical giggle of relief, because when the manager strode over, looking so serious, she thought it was about the pills; that someone had told on her and now she'd be fired on the spot, the police would be called and she'd be caught red-handed with a bag full of pill strips and opioid patches. For she had done exactly what Björn had told her and taken as many pills as she could. While the residents were having lunch down in the refectory, she'd used her master key to gain entry to some of the apartments and rifled through them in search of drugs.

As she left the building, a car pulled up alongside her. It was Björn's brother, Ebbi, who smiled and offered her a lift. She got in the car even though she knew exactly what was coming. But it was such a luxury not to have to take the bus home and walk up the hill to Engihjalli. Especially when her body ached all over.

For a while they drove in silence, but when Ebbi stopped at a traffic light on Sæbraut, he said:

'I'm worried about you, Ísafold.' He glanced at her then looked back at the road ahead.

Ísafold felt her face flush with embarrassment and anger. What business was it of Ebbi's, anyway? Yes, she'd involved him by seeking his help because of Björn, but that didn't make it his concern. She said nothing, simply shrugged her shoulders and stared out of the window. The sea was calm and the tourists milling about the lighthouse looked less hunched against the cold than usual. Maybe spring was on the way.

They didn't speak anymore, though Ísafold felt Ebbi's eyes on her from time to time, as if he were still waiting for her to respond. Or maybe he was staring at the bruise on her cheekbone, which hadn't been visible over the weekend but as the swelling went down had blossomed into a purple flower. No amount of make-up could cover it up completely, not even the theatrical greasepaint she'd bought online, which concealed most things.

After pulling up outside the apartment block, Ebbi switched off the engine and turned to her. Ísafold prayed Björn wasn't looking out of the window just then, because he wouldn't be happy if he saw her talking to Ebbi. And then a lengthy interrogation would ensue.

'You know you can leave him anytime. You can get help. Your mother and Áróra and I are willing to help you get back on your feet.'

Ísafold snorted. 'Not Áróra,' she said, aware of the bitterness in her own voice. 'Áróra says she's had enough of me.'

Ebbi looked at her searchingly. 'Isn't that because whenever she comes running to try to help you, you always go back to Björn for more beatings?'

Ebbi's words hit a raw nerve, and although she knew this was exactly what her father had meant when he said 'the truth hurts the most', it didn't stop her from hissing back at Ebbi:

'Isn't what Björn said true – you just want to break us up because you have a crush on me?'

Ísafold shocked herself with her own words. It was almost as if Björn were talking through her. She could hear the echo of his voice in her head as she spoke.

Ebbi seemed less surprised than she was, but there was a deep sadness in his eyes. 'Maybe I care about you more than I should, but this isn't about that, Ísafold. I'm just afraid that one day...'

Ísafold didn't hear him finish his sentence, because she had bolted out of the car, slamming the door behind her and was striding towards the block. She didn't even greet Ómar, who was busy sweeping the pavement and smiled when he saw her approach. She could feel the anger, tinged with disappointment, boiling inside her. Everyone had their selfish reasons for everything. Friendship was never just friendship. There was always something behind it.

65

When Helena told Gutti she thought it would be best if she joined him in the interrogation of Grímur, Gutti had managed to remain impassive while she listed her reasons: she had got to know Grímur, she and Vala had discovered the clue in the Suðurnes police's log, and she had followed up on the Canada lead that enabled them to rule out Björn having gone to Canada. Gutti snorted at the last part, but nodded at the rest, adding that he'd planned to ask her to partner him in the interrogation. Helena knew this was untrue, because on the system Gutti had already allocated the task to Baldvin, but she let it pass, seeing as how she'd got her own way.

Grímur sat shivering next to his solicitor. Helena could almost hear his teeth chatter, and as she and Gutti sat down she asked him if he was cold.

'Maybe a little,' he murmured, so she stood up and said she'd fetch him a hot drink. Grímur asked for tea but the solicitor declined the offer of a coffee.

Helena opened the door and requested tea and a blanket for Grímur, and a coffee for herself with some sweet biscuits. It never hurt to raise the blood sugar a little.

'We want you to feel comfortable here, Grímur, so you must let us know if there's anything else you need or want.'

Helena smiled genially, but Grímur said nothing, so Gutti began by explaining the interrogation procedure: several other people would be watching via a video link, including a representative from the prosecutor's office.

'Your legal status is now that of witness, and therefore according to the law you're obliged to respond to all our questions clearly and to the best of your knowledge.'

'I've already been through most of this with my client,' the young solicitor said solemnly. He was a duty solicitor the station had brought in to act on behalf of Grímur, who had no idea who to ask for. The man had arrived promptly and quickly got himself up to speed on all the case documents.

'As you're aware,' Helena commenced. 'We're investigating the deaths of Ísafold Jónsdóttir and Björn Árnason, who disappeared in the spring and the early summer of 2018, respectively, and whose bodies were discovered in a crevice in the lava field close to Keflavík Airport earlier this spring.'

'I am aware of that,' Grímur stammered. 'Although I've no idea what any of it has to do with me.'

'You knew both the victims. You live in the same apartment block they lived in at the time they disappeared,' Gutti said.

'Lots of people live there. It's a high-rise.' Grímur spat out the words.

Just then, a young policewoman entered with a blanket and refreshments, so Gutti's response, about them speaking to other neighbours as well, was drowned out amid the kerfuffle of the blanket being spread over Grímur's knees and him being asked if he took milk. Grímur immediately grabbed two biscuits from the plate, as though eager to get some before they disappeared, and began to munch on them.

'Icelandic vanilla creams are much better than any of those foreign biscuits,' he said with his mouth full.

Helena's eyes met Gutti's, who clearly found Grímur's manner even stranger than Helena's description of him. Helena reached for a vanilla cream, munching along with Grímur and smiling contentedly as if she too were a big fan of the biscuits, when in fact she found them weak on the vanilla and far too sweet.

'Tell us about Ísafold,' she said. 'You and she were friends, right?'

'Ísafold was a lovely girl,' said Grímur. 'A lovely woman. You're barking up the wrong tree if you think I could have harmed her. I would never have hurt Ísafold.'

'What about Björn,' Gutti suddenly asked. 'Could you have hurt Björn?'

'Maybe,' said Grímur, and started on another biscuit.

The duty solicitor sat up straight in his chair, as did Helena. She could feel her heart racing in her chest, and all her senses sharpening. Maybe this interrogation would be over sooner than they'd anticipated.

66

At every traffic light, turning and roundabout he navigated on his way home, Daníel rehearsed a fresh version of what he was going to say to Áróra. He had sent her a text message inviting her over to his place, and she'd sent one back to say she was already there. It made him oddly happy that she should use the spare key he'd given her so freely, yet he found himself wondering more and more whether she'd ever give him a key to her apartment. But this wasn't the issue right now.

Now he was going to thank her for the work she'd done looking into Kaffikó's finances, and then make it absolutely clear to her the investigation was over and she must stop thinking about the case. It wasn't complicated; however, he was aware that she'd immersed herself so fully in the task because she needed to keep busy. She needed something to occupy her mind.

He parked the car outside the house, and got out. But instead of going straight inside, he turned to look at the nearby stream and took a few deep breaths. There was a pair of swans on the water and a skein of geese flying above, honking as if to welcome the green tinge slowly extending over everything. He exhaled heavily a few times, before turning on his heel, opening the front door and entering the house.

Áróra was in the kitchen.

'Hi, sweetie!' he called out, taking off his jacket as he walked in. But when Áróra turned around he let his jacket fall to the floor and rushed over to her.

'Áróra! What happened to you?' She had a split lip, a big bump on her forehead, and the bluish-red burn mark on her neck bore the clear pattern of a rope.

'I got into a bit of a scuffle,' she said, and Daníel shook his head frantically.

'Where? Who with? Tell me!' He wanted the whole story.

'I couldn't just sit on my hands, so I paid a visit to Sturla, Kaffikó's investor. And I decided to follow one of his errand boys. He wasn't too happy about me tailing him.'

'And what? Did he just attack you? Did he try to strangle you? Have you any idea who he is, what his name is? Can you describe his appearance?' It was as if Daníel had forgotten all his years of experience in interview techniques. He fired questions at Áróra so fast that she had to place a restraining hand on his arm. Then he calmed down, and gently stroked the red mark on her neck with his finger.

'No, I don't know his name. But he's of average height and build, with a mop of dark curls that falls over his forehead. I don't think he was trying to kill me. He was probably partly defending himself. And, in hindsight, I may have over-reacted a bit. I think I might have knocked him unconscious.'

Daníel picked his jacket up from the floor. 'Come along,' he said. 'We're going to A&E.'

'No, no, no,' protested Áróra. 'I'll put some ice on it.' She raised a bag of frozen vegetables and pressed it to her throat.

'You're going to do as I say,' Daníel declared firmly, taking her hand and pulling her along. 'With any pressure applied to the neck there's a risk of stroke afterwards, so you need to be examined. We're going to the hospital right now.'

Áróra resisted, freed her hand and looked straight at him. He saw the familiar flash of defiance in her eyes, but countered it with his stern face. A moment later she softened and followed him meekly into the hallway, where he bundled her into his thick Icelandic wool sweater and led her out to the car.

'I'll use the trip to A&E to try to find your attacker. From what you've told me there's every chance he's been there himself today,' Daníel said, and dialled the number of the police station on his phone.

'Oh, no,' said Áróra. 'I don't want to deal with all the hassle of filing a report.'

Daníel looked at her, puzzled. 'The guy injured you, Áróra.'

She cleared her throat uneasily. 'His injuries might be worse,' she murmured.

Daníel laughed. 'I don't doubt that,' he said. 'Still, I'm determined to have him found and locked up for the night. It'll do him good.'

67

Helena could barely keep her eyes open as she and Gutti sat with Björn's brother, Ebbi, at their mother, Bryndís's house, waiting for her to prepare the coffee and biscuits they had actually declined. All of her energy had gone into interrogating Grímur, and she would have preferred to go straight home, down a couple of beers and fall asleep in front of the TV with her feet in Sirra's lap. But that wasn't an option. Gutti had decided it was best to get the unpleasant task of talking to Björn's relatives over with.

They had relayed most of what had come up during their interrogation of Grímur, including how he let himself into Ísafold and Björn's apartment, stole his passport and booked a flight in Björn's name on his computer. Grímur was currently remanded in custody at Hólmsheiði prison. However, in the middle of their account Bryndís had suddenly stood up from the sofa and decided to prepare some refreshments. When they made to protest, Ebbi signalled to them to let her get on with it.

'Mum always finds it difficult to hear that Björn was violent towards Ísafold,' Ebbi said. 'She's never wanted to acknowledge that her son was a fucking bully.'

'It's not easy to confront the failings of someone you love,' Helena said. They saw a lot of this in their line of work.

'Is it certain, then, that Björn killed Ísafold?' Ebbi asked after a brief pause.

'Yes,' Gutti replied. 'We have no reason to doubt Grímur's testimony in this regard. We questioned him at length and are satisfied that he's not embellishing his role in all of this. Much of the evidence corroborates his story. There are also other details, which, in the interests of the investigation, we haven't made public yet, but which coincide with Grímur's testimony.'

Gutti rambled on in this vein, and Helena admired the man's ability to talk without saying very much. One thing he didn't tell Ebbi was that Grímur seemed to have no idea that Ísafold's heart was missing. And no matter how they approached the subject, or tried to pressure him, it was obvious that although he knew where Ísafold's body was hidden and when she was killed, he knew nothing about the manner of her death.

'Grímur's full confession to the murder of Björn, together with details he provided that correspond precisely with the pathologist's findings, make it clear that he knows everything about Björn's death, but very little about that of Ísafold,' Gutti wrapped up.

'I still feel bad about the last time I spoke to Ísafold,' Ebbi said then in a hushed voice, and Helena saw he had tears in his eyes. 'When I half confessed my love for her, she looked at me as if I'd betrayed her. Whenever I think about her now, I see that look. And I believe that's why she didn't come to me for help at the end, when perhaps she needed me most.'

'I think it's fair to say there was very little you could have done to save Ísafold,' Gutti said, and Helena knew he was right. Based on her own knowledge of the case, the only person who could have saved Ísafold was herself.

Bryndís now returned with a thermos of coffee, sat down and served them all. Gutti took his cup, leaned back comfortably on the sofa and contemplated mother and son.

'Did you know any of the young men who worked for Björn?'

They shook their heads as one.

'Do the names Jonni, Guðmundur, Felix or Hallur mean anything to you?'

Bryndís shook her head again, but Ebbi nodded.

'I remember Felix,' he said. 'He used to drive Björn around a lot. Mostly when he'd been drinking, I think. Why are you asking about those boys?'

'We're just looking for more witnesses,' Helena replied.

68

Entering the apartment, Ísafold was relieved to hear voices coming from the living room. Björn was in there talking to Felix and Mummi, so he couldn't have seen her get out of Ebbi's car and that saved her a lot of explaining.

Björn looked at her as soon as she entered. 'Hi Ísafold. Bring over the haul.' He patted the coffee table, and Ísafold took a seat in one of the armchairs.

She began to pull the blister strips from her bag under the watchful eyes of the three men, who rummaged through them, and immediately started arranging them according to some system she didn't understand. Then Mummi extracted a pair of nail scissors from his pocket and began to cut some of the strips in half and others into individual pills.

'Oh, gabapentin,' Björn said reproachfully, waving one of the strips in the air. 'You're not supposed to take gabapentin, Ísafold.'

'It's fine,' said Felix. 'I have a customer for it.' He took the strip and put it in his pocket.

'Okay. But we won't include it in our inventory. It's below our lowest price category.'

Felix and Mummi nodded, and suddenly Ísafold found it all so strange. To hear them talk about inventories and price categories in relation to the pills she'd stolen from the elderly. As if this were a normal business transaction. As if Björn were running a small shop that sold normal merchandise. She gave a start when Björn looked at her.

'Is this everything?'

She nodded as she scratched about for the last of the pills in the bottom of her bag. 'Then there are just the patches,' she said. 'I wasn't sure if I should take this many.' She placed them on the table.

Mummi instantly grabbed a handful of them. 'Awesome, fentanyl patches – high-dosage. These things sell like hotcakes. Junkies boil them and shoot up the liquid.'

'Yeah, nice one, Ísafold. Definitely take lots of these,' said Björn. 'Used ones are popular, too, so if you're helping some old fart change their patch, be sure to keep the old one.'

'I think the nurses do that,' Ísafold said in a hushed voice.

She stood up and left the room, took off her coat and put it on a hanger together with her bag. On her way into the bedroom, she overheard Björn telling the lads he'd be on Telegram all evening advertising while they delivered the orders.

She sat on the edge of the bed and gazed into space. She felt as if her mind had crash-landed in a place she'd known about but which still seemed alien to her. She didn't really understand why she was so shocked. What had been staring her in the face all along, and she'd half chosen to ignore, was now clear as day. Björn had stopped trying to pretend, or fob her off with talk of investments, or some harmless business on the side. There was nothing harmless about selling pills. Björn was a drug dealer, plain and simple. Not an investor, or a businessman, or an entrepreneur. All those titles he used to make himself look good were a complete lie. He was a small-time drug dealer who made money from vulnerable addicts.

FRIDAY

69

It wasn't even noon when Björn called the next day.

'How much have you got?' he asked.

Ísafold rushed out into the corridor and spoke in a low voice. Her reaction was almost instinctual, for surely nobody could have guessed what she was talking about on the phone.

'Five,' she said, and heard him groan at the other end of the line. 'Is that all?'

'Yes,' she whispered. 'It's not midday yet. Midday is the best time.'

'Okay,' he breathed. 'Bring out whatever you've got. The boys have already sold everything, so I need more supplies.'

Ísafold gave a start. 'Are you outside?'

'Yes, I'm in the forecourt. Hurry up.'

Ísafold's heart was hammering in her chest and she felt the prickle of sweat on her back.

'Not out front,' she pleaded softly into the phone. 'Someone might see you.'

'So what?' Björn snapped. 'Can't a guy visit his girlfriend at work? Is that so strange? If anyone asks, tell them I forgot the key to the apartment and I came by to pick up yours.'

'All right,' Ísafold whispered. This was the Björn she knew. Afraid of nothing, brimming with confidence and clear-headed. Nothing like the man she'd seen quake with fear over his debt to Sturla. He must have found a way to get the money together.

She darted along the corridor and left the building through a side door rather than using the main entrance directly onto the forecourt, hoping to draw less attention to herself that way. As she slipped into the passenger seat, Björn held out his hand and she

clasped hold of it, only realising when he snickered that she was supposed to place the strips into his upturned palm.

She laughed too. 'Hello, my love,' she said chirpily, and he looked
at her quizzically, the side of his mouth curved in a smile. He was
handsome when he gave that half-smile. It was one of the things
she'd first noticed and been attracted to when they met at the Icelandic Society in London.

'Hi, sweetheart,' he said, leaning forward and kissing her on the
lips. She returned his kiss tenderly, and for an instant they lingered
in that warm intimacy, each breathing in the other's aroma, and
Ísafold felt something inside her melt.

'Sorry it's so little,' she said passing him the strips.

He inspected them then nodded contentedly. 'It's great to get this
much Oxy,' he said.

'And it's not even lunchtime yet,' she replied, feeling emboldened.
More than anything she wanted to please Björn, to help him out of
this predicament so that everything would go better between them.
'How much do you owe Sturla?'

Björn pulled a face. 'That's anyone's guess. This isn't really about
precise amounts; it's more about me giving him a sum he's happy
with. Then I'll be in his good books. I've always tried to stay under
the radar, if you know what I mean, keep my activities low key, and
hope the big-time dealers wouldn't notice me. But that's over now.
So I'm going to sell as much as I can today and tomorrow, then go
to Sturla, give him the money and try to negotiate. Work out a percentage or something.' Björn voice was warm and Ísafold gave him
a parting kiss on the lips.

'I'll do my very best today,' she said, opening the car door to get
out, but Björn grabbed her arm.

'Thanks, Ísafold,' he said. 'We make a great team, don't we?'

Ísafold smiled and nodded, her heart swelling with a feeling of
relief and gratitude for this moment, which she had created – or
rather allowed to happen – by greeting him cheerfully and kissing

him goodbye. She'd probably been too down in the dumps lately. Too anxious and fearful. And that didn't bring out the best in Björn.

70

Helena sipped her coffee between spoonfuls of skyr, and pondered how Sirra always managed to look gorgeous no matter what time of day it was. Even when she woke up she resembled a movie star. Despite being dishevelled, her wavy hair fell prettily about her face, and however crumpled her nightgown was, it somehow creased so perfectly around her shapely body, revealing just enough to make Helena curse the fact she had a work day ahead and not a holiday, which they could have spent in bed.

'What are you up to today, darling?' Sirra asked, browsing the paper and taking a bite of toast.

Helena picked up her phone and opened the work task list Gutti had sent her. 'It seems my schedule involves tracking down a man. A key witness in a case we're working on.'

She didn't mention that it was Áróra's sister's case. She took her duty of confidentiality seriously and seldom breached it, unless she felt a desperate need to unburden her heart. On those rare occasions, she had sometimes given Sirra scraps of information, but she mostly restrained herself. It was a common complaint among the partners of police officers. This secrecy that could be interpreted as a kind of dishonesty, but which was in fact one of the responsibilities of the job.

'How about you?' she asked.

'Not much,' said Sirra. 'Apart from a short course after lunch, I'm having a quiet day.'

The door to the front room opened and Bisi came out.

'*Bonjour*, good morning, *góðan dag*,' she said. She wore a colourful African dress that suited her well and at the same time brightened up the surroundings. Bisi had discovered two stores in Reykjavík that sold African goods, and was making the most of them. There she'd found various ingredients for the meals she prepared for her flatmates, but also dresses, tablecloths, curtains, and other items with which she'd added character to the apartment. Her own room would have borne her unmistakeable mark, too, had Sirra and Helena not persuaded her to decorate every other room except her own, so it wouldn't appear too African, thus giving away the fact that she and not Helena was the occupant. The advice had proved sound, since the immigration people had peeked into all the rooms, as though hoping to find something that would show a breach of the law.

'What's on the agenda for you today, Bisi?' Sirra asked.

Bisi waved her hand dismissively and made a beeline for the pestle and mortar – one of her acquisitions from Afrozone. She set about vigorously grinding cardamom pods, filling the kitchen with their aroma. Then she added a sprinkling to her coffee, as well as a generous amount of sugar, and seemed to enjoy the result.

'Same old same old, working at the till, refilling shelves. It's fine,' Bisi said. 'We're doing stocktaking today, so I won't get home until midnight.'

'Before you know it you'll be store manager,' Helena said, but Bisi gave a shrug.

'It's fine,' she said. 'Someday I'll get a good job here. I've applied to two computer-repair shops – maybe something will come of that.'

Bisi took her coffee and went back to her room. She often disappeared like that to give Helena and Sirra space, and Helena was grateful for that, although sometimes they would coax her out to watch TV or have a chat, when they felt she was spending too much time in her room.

Helena rose to her feet and said goodbye to Sirra, limiting herself to a quick peck on the cheek so she wouldn't regret still more not having the day off. She filled her travel mug, and took it with her out to the car, then drank half the coffee while selecting the music she wanted to listen to on her way to work. This morning routine was Helena's way of gearing herself up for the day ahead, so choosing the right track was crucial. Today she needed something energising but at the same time gentle to get herself going. Yesterday had been emotionally draining, even though she was pleased with the outcome.

All the way down to the station she sang along to 'Super Trouper' at the top of her lungs, and by the time she walked in she felt invigorated and in the best of moods. She drummed the beat of the song on the front desk while submitting a request for Felix Áslaugarson to be brought in for questioning. The duty officer filled out the form but then stared at his computer for a few seconds and said:

'Felix Áslaugarson? He's currently in one of our holding cells. Daniel Hansson asked for him to be arrested last night in A&E.'

71

Helena looked faintly irritated as she stood over Daníel and read him the riot act. He wondered whether her disappointment at finding Felix already in custody was because she'd been looking forward to going on a manhunt.

'Were you hoping for some action?' he asked teasingly, but she seemed in no laughing mood.

'He's injured,' she said. 'Badly injured. And he claims it happened during his arrest yesterday.'

Daníel shook his head. 'You should ask him more about that, because I know for a fact the police didn't beat him up. The reason I had him arrested was because he got involved in...' Daníel paused as he searched for the right words, before settling on Áróra's description of the fight. 'Long story short, he was involved in a scuffle yesterday, and his injuries are a result of the person he assaulted defending themselves.'

'That must have been some defence,' Helena said.

'Yes. The victim was actually my girlfriend, Áróra.'

'That figures,' snorted Helena.

It hadn't escaped Daníel that Helena was a bit wary of Áróra. He couldn't quite work out why, but thought it might stem from Helena's protective instinct towards him. She'd often hinted that she thought Áróra was too wild for him.

'She doesn't plan to press charges,' said Daníel.

'More to the point perhaps is whether *he* plans to press charges,' Helena said. 'I'm sure Áróra doesn't look half as bad as he does.'

Daníel shrugged. 'He tried to strangle her with a piece of cord,' he said, and Helena looked at him, puzzled. 'As I said, it's a long story, but it seems this Felix guy works for Sturla Larsen,

who I'm sure you've heard of. You can ask him about that yourself, because Áróra can't be bothered to make a formal complaint
so I'm handing him over to you. Just promise me you'll keep him
as long as you can, and don't go easy on him, whatever it is you're
going to question him about.'

'Actually, it's in relation to Áróra's sister's case.'

Daníel felt his heart sink to the pit of his stomach, and it
seemed to resound in his head, as if it were hollow inside. 'I see,'
he said softly. He knew better than to probe Helena about it, although he desperately wanted to know whether Felix was a
suspect or a witness. He rose and put on his jacket. 'Good luck,'
he said and walked towards the door.

72

Ísafold cried on her way home on the bus. She sat at the back, leaned her hot forehead against the window and let the tears flow. It wasn't that she hadn't expected to be fired; in fact she'd known it was only a matter of time, even so the shame of it stung. The manager had eyed her sharply and her expression betrayed a sort of contemptuous pity. She told Ísafold she'd been caught on camera entering various apartments at lunchtime. Apartments of residents who weren't under her care. And there had also been reports of drugs missing from the pharmacy. Ísafold sat, eyes downcast, pulse racing, and said nothing. She was expecting the police to burst in at any moment, snatch her bag off her and discover the twelve strips of opioid medication, but no police arrived.

'You needn't come back to work,' the manager told her. Then she turned towards her computer screen, as if she could no longer bear the sight of Ísafold, who remained immobile in her chair, unsure what to do. Whether she was allowed to leave or not.

Finally, she rose tentatively, and as the manager continued to stare at the computer screen it was clear that she meant for Ísafold to go.

As she made her way along Hverfisgata, the cold wind coming in off the sea didn't suffice to cool her face, which was burning with shame. And when she got on the bus at Hlemmur, she could no longer hold back her tears. She had disgraced herself, been fired from her job, and she wouldn't get a reference for another position. Worst of all: Björn was sure to be furious. She just hoped the twelve strips, which for some reason the manager hadn't demanded she hand over, would assuage his anger.

Ísafold barely managed to drag herself up the hill to Engihjalli. It was as if the pull of gravity was stronger that day than on other days, and she had the impression she might suddenly lose the ability to walk upright and roll helplessly back down the hill. As she reached the car park outside the block, she was seized by an uncontrollable urge to call Áróra. But she didn't, because she knew Áróra was sick of all her problems and wanted her to leave Björn and go back to England. What Áróra didn't understand was that for Ísafold that would signify failure. It would go against everything she'd been striving for these past few years; all her efforts to make Iceland her home, to connect with the country of her father, would have been pointless. She would crawl back there, mouthing some pathetic excuses about why the Icelandic adventure hadn't worked out.

It was a relief that Björn didn't get angry. He was delighted with the strips and took Ísafold in his arms, mumbling something about how she could just find another job. She sobbed on his chest, gradually letting herself be comforted. His deep voice and soothing whispers calmed her, and soon she felt that maybe it wasn't as bad as all that. Björn was right when he said that it could have been a lot worse. The manager could have called the police. She could have confiscated the pills. So, actually, Ísafold had got off lightly.

'We'll sell all these tonight,' Björn said, setting the strips on the kitchen table. 'And tomorrow I'll go and pay Sturla.'

73

'What the hell happened to you?' Agla said, as soon as Áróra stepped into her office.

She wore a turtleneck top to conceal the red mark on her throat, but the bump on Áróra's forehead now looked considerably more dramatic, the bruise having extended to her eyebrow and acquired a purple hue. Nor was there any way of hiding her split lip.

'I got into a scuffle with one of the errand boys who works for a guy named Sturla Larsen,' Áróra explained. Agla looked at her blankly. Obviously, she'd never heard of the man. 'Sturla Larsen is the investor who bailed out Kaffikó a year after the company was set up, and he's been using it ever since to launder money.'

Now Agla perked up. 'Aha,' she said, gesturing to Áróra to take a seat. 'Do you have documentary evidence?' she asked, pragmatic as ever.

Áróra handed her the folder with the summary she'd prepared that morning. 'A simple comparison shows that Kaffikó has far bigger revenues than the other coffeehouse chains, although their outgoings are similar. And, if you examine the accounts in the random audit you conducted, you'll see that a far higher percentage of Kaffikó's takings is in cash, the majority of it in foreign currency. The other chains don't receive nearly as much cash or foreign currency, even though their branches are located close to popular tourist spots. Yesterday, I tailed one of Sturla's errand boys as he went on his rounds between coffeehouses – a bag under his arm – to do the cashing up. So, it's pretty obvious that Kaffikó's owners, Gyða and Marteinn, have been laundering money through their company for their so-called investor.

Whether they've done so willingly or not is unclear, but this Sturla is a known drug baron with suspected links to international criminal gangs.'

'That's quite something,' Agla said, leafing distractedly through the documents. 'But it'll be difficult to prove. It's easy to inflate how many cups of coffee you sell, which is why catering companies are generally a total nightmare to investigate.'

'And therefore, perfect for money-laundering.'

'Indeed.' Agla closed the folder and leaned back in her chair. 'I don't really know what we can do with this, but I'll give it some thought.'

'I'm not asking a huge fee for the information,' Áróra said. 'Maybe two million kronur?'

'I just don't see how we'll get any revenue out of this,' Agla said. 'The problem with chasing laundered money, is that the money launderers pay their taxes.'

'Might you try to collaborate with Narcotics to trace the origin of the money Sturla brings into the business?' Áróra said encouragingly, but Agla sighed.

'It's a good idea, but cases like this don't bring in much revenue for the Tax Office, as the police usually confiscate drug money.'

'Won't it all end up in the state coffers anyway, whatever route it takes?'

'Yes,' Agla replied. 'But I'd rather take on cases that boost the figures in our annual financial report. That's what they hired me to do here.'

Now it was Áróra's turn to sigh. 'Christ,' she breathed, unable to conceal her disappointment.

'Alas,' said Agla. 'All that glitters is not gold.'

74

The TV was on but Ísafold had difficulty concentrating on the Eurovision semi-final, even though she'd always loved the show. She had got that from her dad. Every year in mid-May, the festive spirit would seize him, as it did all Icelanders, and he'd prepare an enormous barbecue and then try to invite people. But the Brits didn't get nearly as excited about Eurovision as the Icelanders. As the years went by, he gave up inviting people round, and it was usually just the four of them, installed on the sofa wearing their special Eurovision outfits and trying to guess how many points each contestant would receive. Normally, Ísafold would have called Áróra that evening and chatted about the competition. They would have discussed at length the Icelandic entry, taken bets on which contestant would do best in each group. Laughed together. But she and Áróra weren't on speaking terms. And tonight Ísafold's nerves were on edge – she couldn't concentrate on anything, because Björn had gone to pay Sturla and to try to negotiate with him over percentages.

Ísafold paced the room, pondering all the things Björn had told her about Sturla. That he was dangerous. That he'd killed two men and got away with it. That he was known to torture people who crossed him. What emerged from this deluge of thoughts was an image of Björn sitting tied to a chair, while Sturla and the two tracksuited men beat him up. The thought of this made Ísafold's stomach churn, and she had to fight back the tears. For all Björn's mistreatment of her, she couldn't bear to think of him being hurt. So what if that meant she loved him more than he loved her, like Áróra said, she didn't care. All that mattered was that she loved him. This had become clear to her in recent days. Her man was in trouble and she wanted to stand by him. Regardless of everything that had happened before.

She went to the window once more and looked out at the car park. Still no sign of Björn's car. She was bursting for the toilet so she went into the bathroom. She had scarcely come back out when the front door opened and Björn walked in. He was unharmed. At least, she couldn't see any obvious injuries.

'How did it go?' she said excitedly. 'Are you okay?'

He shrugged. 'Yeah,' he said. 'Everything's fine.'

Her relief was so overwhelming that she flung her arms about him and hugged him violently. But Björn didn't return her embrace, merely gave her a little pat on the back before pushing her away. He was sweating, and seemed strangely jittery.

'What's wrong?' she asked, puzzled.

'Nothing,' he replied. 'Everything's fine. Just give me some space.' He hung up his jacket then massaged his forehead between his eyebrows.

Bewildered, Ísafold followed him into the kitchen. Had he been snorting cocaine with Sturla? Did that mean they were friends now? Or had the meeting gone so badly that Björn had decided to cheer himself up with a few snorts afterwards?

'Was Sturla satisfied with the money?' she asked.

'Not exactly,' he replied. 'He wants a bigger sacrifice.'

'Like what?'

'Stop asking questions, woman! Leave me alone!' Björn's voice quavered, and he had that wild look in his eyes that Ísafold knew well, and which wasn't a good sign. The best thing for her now would be to retreat. In fact, she should probably leave the apartment immediately.

Björn opened a kitchen drawer and rummaged through it, as if he were going to get himself something to eat and was looking for the cheese slicer, but then he leaned forward over the counter, shoulders hunched, his back to her. Was he crying? Ísafold approached him cautiously and placed her hand on his shoulder.

'My darling Ice-Bear,' she said. 'What's wrong?'

He gave a start, and because she expected a blow to the face the stab in her side caught her by surprise. She stared straight at Björn as though frozen, and he stared back at her, yet his face betrayed fear rather than cruelty, which made everything even more incomprehensible. Then came another stab, and another, and yet another, but still Ísafold didn't connect them to the kitchen knife in Björn's hand. Then it dawned on her, and she pushed him away, ran into the bathroom, and locked herself inside.

She sat with her back against the door, pushing back against his blows. First he pounded then he kicked, and finally he threw his whole weight at the door, until she felt the frame give way.

She screamed with every ounce of strength in her body and soul, but she knew this time it would do no good. For it was almost certain that in every single apartment in the block the music was on full blast. Tonight was the first semi-final of Eurovision and Iceland was competing.

75

It was every detective's dream to solve a murder case, get to the bottom of a set of mysterious events, close out an investigation. That was why Helena was so surprised at herself; her body seemed to be responding to the experience with fatigue. She opened her second can of energy drink, as she couldn't face another coffee, but it was actually the sugar keeping her going now. She crammed another handful of chocolate-covered raisins into her mouth. She had always thought she'd be bursting with energy and enthusiasm at this point in a case; perhaps she was sliding into middle age.

Felix had requested a bathroom break, which she and Gutti had gladly granted. Gutti because he needed to stretch his back, and Helena because she needed another caffeine and sugar fix. She was back in the interview room when Felix and his solicitor returned. She sat up straight and tidied her hair – she was aware that everyone involved in the case was now following the interview online, both here at the station and at the prosecutor's office. She had to keep reminding herself not to slouch in her seat as she had a tendency to do.

'I've decided I won't name the big guy I told you about,' Felix said as he sat down. 'From now on I'll just call him "the big guy", okay?'

Helena felt like giving a loud sigh of dismay, and had the impression Gutti felt the same way. Apparently it was the rule rather than the exception that the big guys got away while the small fry paid for their crimes. It hadn't taken long, though, to put two and two together and figure out that the big guy Felix was talking about was Sturla Larsen; however, unless he named him, they had no evidence. They had tried to put pressure on

Felix, threatened to charge him in connection with the assault on Áróra, but he'd stood his ground, and now, after speaking with his solicitor, he seemed doubly determined to keep his mouth shut.

'Of course, we know it's Sturla Larsen we're talking about here,' Helena said. 'And we will summon him for an interview to hear what he has to say about all this.'

Felix shrugged. 'I have nothing to say about that, and my legal counsel here' – Felix pointed his thumb at the solicitor – 'can confirm that I haven't named any names.'

Gutti now huffed noisily and leafed through his notebook, covered in scrawl that was indecipherable to everyone but him.

'Tell us more about Björn's dealings with the big guy,' he said, and Helena had the impression Felix perked up, though it was difficult to read his expression because his face was so swollen and his nose looked disproportionately large, his eyes like two slits amidst the reddish-blue puffiness. For all that, he seemed almost to enjoy recounting what had happened, and it occurred to Helena that maybe it came as a relief to him. People often felt relieved when they shared something that had been weighing on their conscience. She'd seen this clearly yesterday when Grímur let it all out.

76

'The big guy was vile to Björn,' Felix said. 'Of course, he was just taunting him when he said he wanted to eat his girlfriend's heart. Acting the big macho. But Björn was so terrified of him he took him at his word. I drove him over to Stu—' The lawyer gave him a swift jab with his elbow. '...To the big guy's place with...' He paused and cleared his throat. 'With the heart. That was the first time I met the big guy, but I could tell from the smirk on his face when he took the plastic Tupperware box that he had no idea there was a real human heart inside. I guess he thought Björn had gone to the butcher's and bought a pig's heart or liver or something and put it in the box. Who would have thought he would actually kill his girlfriend?' Felix threw his hands up and looked searchingly at the company, but nobody answered.

Gutti on the other hand was ready with the next question. 'And how did the big guy react when he discovered it was a real heart?'

'He wasn't happy,' said Felix. 'He accused Björn of trying to implicate him in a murder, but Björn had completely lost it and argued that the big guy had ordered him to do this. Then they shouted at each other and Björn tried to lunge at Stu— ... the big guy, when the big guy yelled at Björn not to come anywhere near him with the murder victim's DNA. Then the whole thing descended into chaos and the big guy's boys had to intervene.'

Felix flailed his arms about wildly as he described the sequence of events, and Gutti took notes while Helena placed a hand over her ear so she could hear the voice now speaking to her through the headphones. It was Oddsteinn from the prosecutor's office.

'What happened to the heart?' he said.

Helena posed the question, only more indirectly. 'What was the upshot of the fight at the big guy's house?' Felix looked at her blankly, so she rephrased the question. 'How did the fight end?'

Felix nodded. 'The big guy told Björn to go home, get rid of the body and never show his face again, but he gave me the heart, ordered me to dispose of it and bring the box back so he could burn it. I don't think he trusted Björn with the fingerprints. The big guy's smart that way.'

'And was this when you first began working for Sturla Larsen?' Helena felt like kicking Gutti under the table for his clumsy attempt to trick Felix into talking out of turn, even at the cost of destroying the trust they'd built up with him during the interview. And sure enough, Felix clammed up.

'Who says I'm working for Sturla Larsen? I haven't mentioned his name.'

The lawyer looked reprovingly at Gutti, who winked at him companionably, as if this had been some sort of prank. Helena quickly jumped into the role of good cop, and hoped Gutti would take the hint and behave himself.

'Who you work for now is neither here nor there,' she said. 'What we're more interested to know is why you were there, Felix. You say you drove Björn over to the big guy's place, but didn't you find it strange when Björn came out to your car carrying a heart in a plastic box?'

'No, it wasn't like that,' Felix said.

'So, how was it, then?' Helena asked.

'I was the one who helped him cut out her heart.'

77

Björn had been drenched in sweat and shaking all over when Felix arrived. He'd been able to tell from Björn's voice when he called that it was urgent, and he'd repeatedly insisted Felix must go there alone. He was therefore ready some kind of trouble, but nothing could have prepared him for what awaited him in Björn's bathroom. Strewn on the floor were several blood-soaked towels, and in the tub Ísafold's bloodless body lay slouched in the water that streamed constantly from the tap and out through the plughole, having taken on a pinkish tinge.

Felix's knees nearly gave way, and he staggered backward, making as if to flee, but Björn blocked his way.

'You have to help me take her heart out, Felix. Now!'

Felix tried to thrust Björn aside, but Björn pushed him back until they were both inside the bathroom and then Björn shut the door behind them.

'That maniac Sturla wants her heart now, otherwise he's going to kill me. And possibly everyone who's been working for me, too.'

Felix's head was spinning. What the hell was the man talking about? Had he gone raving mad?

'What the fuck happened?' Felix murmured.

Björn slapped him hard on the back of the head. 'This is no time for bullshit,' he said. 'We need to remove her heart now and give it to Sturla today or I'm a dead man, okay? That's the situation and you have to help me.'

Felix struggled to collect his thoughts, which were flying in all directions, whirling round in his head. Only days ago he'd chatted with Ísafold – she'd passed him an orange drink from the fridge – and now there she lay, seemingly lifeless.

'Is she ... dead?' he breathed, and Björn gave him another slap on the back of his head.

'Of course she's fucking dead, you idiot, how else do you think I would cut out her heart?'

Felix approached the bathtub tentatively, as though half expecting her to suddenly move or sit up or say something. But her eyes, which were staring straight at the ceiling, were dull rather than shiny, so he was fairly sure she was dead. He leaned over her anyway and lowered his hand into the water, which he expected to find cold but it was warm. He placed a finger on her neck to check for a pulse and he heard Björn grunt behind him.

'She's fucking dead, Felix. I've kept her in hot water for two hours to drain the blood out of her. Now you need to cut her open and get the heart.'

Felix recoiled, wiping his hand on his trousers. 'No way am I slicing her up, man! Are you crazy?' Felix had blurted this out automatically, and with more vehemence than he could ever have imagined showing Björn.

Björn appeared equally taken aback and the two men stood staring at each other an instant. Then Björn stammered:

'Okay ... okay. All right, then. I'll do it. I'll do it.'

He shuffled his feet and kicked away the blood-soaked towels. Kneeling beside the tub, he pulled open Ísafold's blouse, exposing her naked torso. There were at least three stab wounds, and at the base of her neck a bluish mark that resembled a bruise. Björn lowered his head and emitted a sobbing sound then rose to his full height and looked at Felix.

'Okay,' Felix said. 'I'll do it, but you google and tell me how. Okay? You guide me, right? Google how to take a heart out whole.'

78

Daníel stood on the steps of Áróra's house. He had a bag containing an Indian takeaway, another containing a bottle of wine, and a bunch of flowers in his arms. The moment he'd been waiting for and at the same time dreading had finally arrived.

'I should get around to having a key cut for you,' Áróra said cheerfully as she opened the door. 'It's ridiculous always having to open the door to you like a butler.'

Daníel grinned as he stepped inside, but it was clear that Áróra could read his expression, the way she always did, because she looked concerned.

'What is it?' she said.

There was no reason to drag this out. 'I have news about your sister's case,' he said. 'Gutti and I agreed I should break it to you first, and then tomorrow he'll inform you officially. If you're happy with that.'

She nodded and walked into the living room, where she turned round and stood gazing at him in silence.

'Is this really the end of it all?' she asked.

'Yes,' he said. He set the bags on the kitchen island, pulled out the bottle of white wine, opened it, and filled two glasses he took from the cupboard. Then he looked for a vase for the flowers but couldn't find one so he grabbed the water jug, arranged the flowers in it and put it on the coffee table.

'Your sister's neighbour, Grímur, has confessed to murdering Björn out of revenge for what he did to her.'

Daníel had expected an instant flood of questions, but Áróra said nothing. She simply sat down on the sofa and nodded, digesting the information.

'Gutti will be able to give you the exact date soon – he's

working on extracting more details from Grímur. But it appears that one night in early June, Grímur witnessed Björn leave the building with a large suitcase, which he struggled to lift into the boot of his car. This, together with Björn's history of violence, led Grímur to suspect that the suitcase contained your sister's body. However, instead of calling the police, Grímur followed Björn's car all the way to the Reykjanes peninsula, where he parked off the road and ran back to where he could see Björn drag the suitcase across the ground and throw it into a fissure in the lava. After Björn had left, Grímur climbed down into the fissure, opened a corner of the suitcase and saw a hand. Then he knew his suspicions were true. He told us that he'd slipped Ísafold's engagement ring off her finger to keep as a souvenir because he was very fond of your sister. Naturally, Gutti asked him why he hadn't called the police after discovering her body in the suitcase. Grímur simply said he didn't consider a full life sentence, even if it went to eighteen years, enough of a punishment for Björn. Especially as most people only serve two-thirds of their time inside. Grímur says he thought the matter over for several weeks, and it was only when he noticed Björn had hooked up with another young woman that he decided to put his plan into action and kill Björn before he could begin abusing the new girlfriend.'

Daníel fell silent for a moment and contemplated Áróra. She was sitting still and listening. The only sign of any emotion was a slight tremor in her hand as she held her glass of wine.

Daníel resumed his account.

'So, Grímur managed to lure Björn into his apartment one evening, and when he was there, he hit him on the head with a heavy statue then cut his throat. He crammed Björn's body into a suitcase, just like Björn did with Ísafold, and drove it out to the Reykjanes peninsula, where he threw it into the same lava fissure. There have been earthquakes there for years now, so the suitcase containing Björn dropped down below the one containing Ísafold, which is why we found that one first.'

'And her heart?' Áróra asked at last. 'What about her heart?' Her voice was a hoarse whisper.

'We have found out what happened to it,' Daníel said gently and paused again before continuing. 'It seems Björn had got himself into trouble. He was, as you suspected, a small-time drug dealer. More precisely, he sold prescription meds, or rather his errand boys sold them for him. He acquired the meds either by buying them directly from elderly people or having Ísafold steal them from her workplace. He didn't seem interested in moving into the big league; he made enough money not to have to work too hard and to be able to afford a few luxuries. Still, he eventually attracted the attention of big shots in the business, and once that happened, they put the screws on him. According to our witness, this dealer – whom no one dares mention by name, but who we of course know is Sturla Larsen – enjoys cultivating a badass image. He thinks it strikes fear into everyone around him.'

Áróra placed a restraining hand on Daníel's arm. 'Sturla Larsen? The same Sturla Larsen I was looking into, and who's been squeezing Kaffikó?'

Daníel nodded. 'Sturla decided to torment Björn a bit, and ordered him to bring him his girlfriend's heart as a kind of test. Our witness said he believed Sturla was only joking but that Björn was too crazy to see that. So when Björn showed up at Sturla's with the heart in a plastic box everyone assumed it was an animal's heart and they fell about laughing. But when Björn insisted it was his girlfriend's actual heart, all hell broke loose. Sturla and his crew realised the seriousness of the situation they'd got themselves into. These guys have no scruples about beating people up, but most of them draw the line at murder. Mostly because the attention it brings is bad for business.'

'What did they do with her heart?' Áróra whispered now.

Daníel reached for her hand and clasped it in his. 'Our witness, who told us all this, was tasked with getting rid of it, so he took it out to the beach at Grótta and threw it in the sea.'

Áróra contemplated Daníel for a moment, but asked no more questions. She drew a deep breath then exhaled, slowly and calmly, and it was as if the tension in her body had been released. She sank down on the sofa, curling up into a foetal position.

'I'm going to close my eyes for a while,' she said.

Daníel reached for the blanket and spread it over her. Then he sat by her feet and sipped his white wine, while he gently patted the blanket.

79

She is floating up near the ceiling, light as a balloon, hollow inside, drifting freely, as if the merest gust might sweep her through the open window into the bright June night. Below her on the bathroom floor lies the body, sliced open down the middle so the chest cavity resembles a colourful butterfly alighted on a blood-red flower. Slowly the flower swells and spreads, its petals unfurl, find their way along the grouting between the tiles, until they fill every available space. The whole bathroom floor is red and glistening, and Ísafold tries to understand why her body is lying there in the blood while she herself is floating about in the air.

Next, she's in a car. She is sitting in the back seat. Björn is driving and weeping loudly. With great sobbing breaths. She wants to ask him what's wrong, but nothing comes out. Words are no longer within her grasp. She is a balloon, a seedpod, a dandelion clock, air. A weightless, drifting vapour. She looks down at her knees but there are no knees. No feet, no belly. She has no body. And then she remembers the butterfly on the bathroom floor and realises she's no longer there. She is here in the air. In the back of the car. The roof prevents her from floating up to the sky.

She has escaped through the open window and is floating upward, curling high into the sky like smoke when Björn's weeping calls her back down. She is with Björn once more, and hears the scraping sound as he drags the suitcase across the lava and cries. She knows her body is in the suitcase, but she doesn't care. This is his problem. He has to drag the suitcase. Not her. She is free to float as she pleases, and it's good to be so light and empty inside.

Once more the sound of weeping calls her down. Only now it's not Björn, but her friend. The friend from downstairs who often helped her. Who banged on the door when the noise was at its worst, and who called the police. The friend who gave her a shoulder to cry on. Whom she could trust. And now he is crying for her. He unzips the suitcase, and pulls out a hand, which he kisses. Her hand. He says he loves her and he weeps. She wants to comfort him, to stroke his bald head and tell him everything's all right, but she no longer has words so she says nothing. He scrambles back out of the hole in the lava and walks away. She floats up, high up, sees the red suitcase down inside the fissure and watches Grímur dwindle into the distance. She goes after him, chasing him like a tamed raven hopping between stones then letting the wind catch its wings and lift it. Grímur walks down the gully where he has left his car. He climbs in and contemplates something he is holding in his palm. It is gold, and because it glitters she feels compelled to take it, greedy like the raven, because this is her gold. This is her ring. But Grímur slips the ring in his pocket, turns the car around and drives away. She wants to follow him, follow the gold, but the suitcase pulls her back. She glimpses it deep inside the dark fissure, red and cheerful yet alien amid the black lava, and she knows her dead body lies there, her bloodless butterfly body. Yet she feels no regret, for her only wish is to float. To float higher and higher, up into the light, and there's nothing to stop her now. Nobody is weeping. Nobody is calling her back, and she allows herself to dissolve into myriad tiny particles that break apart and disperse the higher she ascends. Above her, the bright, airy summer light awaits, and Ísafold unravels and dissolves. Leaving her body behind in the deep, dark fissure, black as death.

80

Áróra jogged slowly west, away from the city centre, feeling the heaviness in her head evaporate in the cool air. It was a bright spring night and the city slept, although it was a wonder anyone could sleep through the din of migrating birds busily nesting and laying their eggs. Áróra hadn't slept much herself. At some point in the late evening, she'd drifted off on Daníel's shoulder in bed, but had awoken soon after, and lain there unable to get back to sleep. She had gazed into space, reflecting, allowing the images of her sister's sad fate to float freely in her mind, allowing them to wound and injure as they whirled round in their finality. The uncertainty was over. She knew exactly how Ísafold's death had occurred, and what people said was true: it was better to know. And although it had been tough to listen to Daníel's account, it was a relief that the uncertainty was over. Daníel had offered to call her mother the evening before. Áróra hadn't felt up to it herself; she preferred to wait until they could discuss things face to face. There was so much they needed to talk about. So many things they needed to reconcile.

She gave a start when she encountered two foreign tourists dragging suitcases behind them. She stared at the suitcases, then collected herself, they were just carry-on suitcases and the couple were probably on a weekend getaway to Iceland with some budget airline whose flights landed in the early hours.

Áróra jogged past them, mumbled good morning, even though it was still night, then, picking up her pace she broke into a sprint. She slowed down, as she approached Grótta, as if her steps were becoming heavier. Finally, she trudged towards the peninsula, where the high tide prevented her from getting out onto the island. She remembered coming here as a child, with her dad and Ísafold. The two sisters had frolicked on the sand, gathering various objects from the shore to show to their dad. He had named their finds – sea creatures, shells and seaweed; he was always bound to the earth, connected to nature, like a big solid rock, rooted in this rugged landscape.

Áróra gazed out at the lighthouse. Above her the artic terns seemed displeased with her arrival and made several attempts to peck her head, but she waved her arms in the air and scared them off. Somewhere along this shoreline, a young man named Felix had thrown Ísafold's heart into the sea, a young man who had later put a cord round her neck. She'd given him a good beating, but would have laid into him still more had she known about this business with Ísafold's heart in the plastic box. Maybe on this very rock he had crouched to rinse out the container, scrub it with a handful of sand before returning it to Sturla, who burned it in the incinerator in his garden.

Somewhere here in the sea the lost part of Ísafold had hidden for a while, but now she'd gone. The sea creatures had long since dissolved her heart, broken it down cell by cell, transformed it into food for other creatures, which themselves would become food for the shellfish that became food for the fish that were in turn devoured by the seals that swam about this island, only coming ashore to nurse their young, or to bask briefly in the sun. Or even by whales which, not content to remain in Icelandic waters, navigated the world's oceans. So, somewhere, perhaps near the South Pole, there was a tiny fragment of Ísafold that had become a part of the planet's ecosystem, rising and falling with the phases of the moon, the ebb and flow of the tides. Her heart beat in rhythm with the waves on all the shores of all the countries in the world.

Áróra bent down and dipped her hands in the sea. She filled her cupped palms, brought them up and immersed her face in the salty water. She sipped, filled her mouth, then spat. She scooped up more water, rubbed her eyes until they stung then ran her fingers through her hair. Seized by a sudden impulse, she stripped off her clothes and stepped into the ice-cold sea. Gradually the water encircled her, first up to her knees then her hips, the sharp stones pricking the soles of her feet. She swam a few strokes until she began to shiver uncontrollably and felt her heart beating hard in her chest. Then she turned back and swam as fast as she could to the shore. She crawled up onto the beach quaking with cold, cramp in her jaw, teeth chattering. She pulled on her tracksuit bottoms and stuffed her knickers into her pocket. It was a struggle getting her T-shirt and sweater on while she was still wet, and she had to sit down to brush the sand off her feet and put on her shoes. Then she jogged home.

Her body suddenly became burning hot and her face felt flushed, the salt drying on her skin making it itch. Her search was over. Ísafold's fate had been revealed, and for the first time since she received the fateful phone call when her mother told her that her sister had disappeared, Áróra felt able to breathe fully, deep down into the bottom of her lungs, so that the oxygen flowed through her veins, to her muscles and her heart. She was free. She didn't need to be there. Nothing bound her to Iceland. Her sister was in the sea and embraced the whole world. She would follow Áróra always, wherever she went.

THREE WEEKS LATER

81

'I'm here to cash up,' Felix said, entering the last coffeehouse of the day.

He'd almost slipped back into his normal life these past few weeks. The investigation into Ísafold's death and his part in it was ongoing, but his solicitor was of the opinion that the charges against him would be relatively minor – obstruction of justice or the like. And anyway, after all this time the police would struggle either to corroborate the story he'd told them about Ísafold, or refute it. So for now he was free, simply under investigation. Sometimes he was thankful to live in Iceland. In other countries he would be in prison, on remand, while the police took their time searching for evidence against him.

Carlos the barista nodded, jiggling his grey curly hair. 'Go ahead,' he said, moving away from the cash register.

Felix liked Carlos. He didn't try to engage him in chit-chat, and never asked any questions. He simply prepared a coffee for him when he arrived and passed it to him in a paper cup on his way out. This coffeehouse was rather quiet, as were most of the others, although today there was a couple at a table over by the window trying to persuade their child to sit still, and a middle-aged man was ensconced in an armchair in the corner with a laptop on his knees.

Felix entered the amounts Sturla had written on a piece of paper into the cash register, printed out the total, tore the strip off and took it with him into the back room. In the corner stood the safe, the same as in the other coffeehouses, a small, green iron lump bolted to the floor. Felix opened it and pulled out Friday's cash bag, which was still there because Kaffikó couldn't be bothered to pay Securitas for a weekend collection. He cut the seal on the bag, but instead of adding banknotes to it as he was supposed to, he emptied the contents into his backpack, which was already quite full, containing, as it did, two lots of daily takings from seven coffeehouses. He had to push down the notes to be able to zip it up. Felix then went to the shelf to fetch two new seals and closed both Friday's and Saturday's bags, both of which would go empty with the Securitas truck to the bank on Monday. There the seals would be broken, and only then would it be discovered that Felix had made off with two days' takings from eight Kaffikó coffeehouses. Or, more precisely, two days' worth of foreign currency that the eight coffeehouses were supposed to have laundered. Felix estimated, based on the usual day's takings, that each cash-up consisted of around half a million Icelandic kronur, so that right now his backpack contained between seven and eight million Icelandic kronur, or between 55,000 and 60,000 dollars.

He closed the safe, scrambled the numbers on the combination lock and slung his backpack over his shoulder. On his way out, Carlos handed him a small paper cup.

'*Un cortado*,' said Carlos.

'*Gracias, señor*,' replied Felix. This had become their routine, after a brief exchange in which Carlos told Felix he was Spanish, and Felix said he loved Spanish coffee. The bitter taste had something to do with the sugar used in the bean roasting process, Carlos had explained enthusiastically, but Felix hadn't committed this fact to memory. However, the cortado on his way out had become the norm whenever Felix came to cash up.

Felix glanced about furtively as he crossed the street and got into his car. He placed the coffee cup in the holder between the seats, and stuffed the backpack down into the footwell, next to his other backpack, which contained a change of jeans and T-shirt, a toothbrush, his passport and pre-paid credit cards he'd linked to his PayPal account, and which now contained all his savings from the years he worked for Sturla.

And it was Sturla who had actually forced him into this. Ever since the incident at Hvolsvöllur, when Sturla had the bag of money stolen from him to fabricate a debt of tens of millions of krónur against him, Felix had felt a sort of defiance brewing inside him. And he realised that if he didn't take control of his life, he would one day explode like a powder keg, with unforeseeable consequences.

Something else probably also influenced his decision: it was reported on the news a few days earlier that a man completely unconnected to Sturla had killed Björn. A neighbour of Björn's who had apparently been friends with Ísafold. Felix felt emboldened to discover that the rumours about Sturla having had Björn killed were false, and in fact there were no confirmed accounts of him killing anyone else either. No doubt it was part of the personal myth Sturla had built around himself, and which Felix himself had propagated among the small-time dealers from whom he collected debts. Fear was such a good way to control people. Better even than money. But Felix was sick and tired of fear.

He had felt afraid ever since he started working for Sturla. His first tasks had been easy, but then Sturla had given him the role of intimidating people. And he just did as he was told, without necessarily knowing why Sturla considered the people he was assigned to harass deserving of punishment. Felix had lasted in this role for several months, and become quite good at throwing rocks through peoples' windows and leaving bloody animal entrails on their doorsteps. But when Sturla told him to kill the dog, he had hesitated and asked why. Then

Sturla told him tens of millions of kronur were at stake if the dog's owners didn't do what he wanted. Felix had, of course, long since realised that the people whose car he keyed, and whose window he smashed, and who still hadn't agreed to comply fully with Sturla's wishes, were the owners of Kaffikó: Marteinn and Gyða.

After the incident with the dog, Felix's fear had spiralled. People who killed animals to intimidate their owners into doing what they wanted weren't good people. Right now, though, Felix was more afraid than he'd ever been. Freedom was in sight, but if Sturla caught him, he'd be in serious hot water. He took deep belly breaths, slow and calm, to try to prevent his anxiety getting the better of him. After all that trouble with the police, Felix noticed that for a while Sturla had someone following him when he went to cash up. However, for several days now he hadn't seen anyone tailing him, and even if someone was watching him, he'd already announced to Sturla he was going on a short break to Amsterdam to party with some friends, to make the most of the time he had, while the police were deciding what exactly to charge him with. So if they saw him drive out to Keflavík everything would be fine.

What he hadn't told Sturla, or anyone else, was that after a layover in Amsterdam he would fly on to Spain, where a rental car was waiting for him. He would then drive to some remote location, some place with a beach where he could swim in the sea and be at peace. Thankfully the police hadn't seen fit to take his passport away from him.

He turned onto Reykjanesbraut and glanced once more in the rear-view mirror. He saw nothing of interest. He settled back in his seat, put on his playlist and smiled to himself. He had created the list especially for this occasion, and it started with the beautifully melodious Abba song that had been a big favourite of his mother's: '*Hasta Mañana*'. Felix picked up the paper cup and drank the bitter coffee in one gulp. Then he sighed contentedly and drummed on the steering wheel in time with the music. Ahead, the grey road snaked through the grey drizzle. But tomorrow he would be basking in sun and heat.

82

Áróra stared out of the car window and watched the flat landscape go by. There was no view of the mountains, as a dense grey
drizzle hung in the air, and Daníel had the windscreen wipers
on nonstop. She had grown so familiar with the Suðurnes peninsula, knew its every nook and cranny, yet now she felt nothing
but sorrow as they glided through the endless lava field.

Daníel gripped the wheel tightly. So tightly his knuckles
showed white. He stared straight ahead at the road, jaw
clenched, but Áróra knew it was only because he wanted to
avoid looking at her. He didn't want their eyes to meet for fear
he'd become emotional. She wanted to reach out and place her
hand gently on his arm, remind him that they hadn't taken a
decision. They hadn't decided to end their relationship, even if
she was planning to relocate to Edinburgh for a while.

The weeks after Ísafold's case was resolved, Áróra had come
to realise that nothing tied her to Iceland except Daníel, and the
feeling that she should stay there because of him somehow oppressed her. Iceland itself oppressed her.

Her apartment seemed empty, and for the first time the
summer drizzle got on her nerves. She kept catching herself
thinking about Edinburgh, her life there before Ísafold disappeared. She found it cosier at Daníel's place – he was so happy
in his little apartment, bickering with Lady Gúgúlú, or Róbert
– who seemed to have moved back into the garage – about
where in the garden his hens could and couldn't roam. At the
same time she craved adventure. She longed to travel, to chase
money in foreign countries – far more substantial amounts than
she could ever hunt down in Iceland. There simply wasn't
enough for her to do here. She had explained this to Daníel, and

he understood. He said he'd always known she needed bigger challenges.

And they had quarrelled. Not immediately after Ísafold's case concluded; Daníel had stifled his resentment for a few days until Áróra had had time to recover. But then he blew up, accused her of having intended to sell confidential information he'd entrusted to her. Áróra didn't know how Daníel had found out about her conversations with Agla at the Directorate of Tax Investigations, nor did it really matter. She tried to explain her point of view, and he his, but to no avail.

'If the Directorate of Tax Investigations had taken on the case, Europol's potential money-laundering investigation would have been reduced to a simple case of tax law violation in Iceland. And Sturla Larsen could just sit back and laugh,' Daníel had said.

'No,' Áróra had argued. 'He would have been forced to cough up. That's what these guys hate most, having to part with their money.'

'No, absolutely not!' Daníel had cried. 'It's the humiliation that gets to them, which is why we need to prosecute them and lock them up.'

Thus, the quarrel had continued. Repeatedly and without any conclusion. Without them being able to reach a shared understanding of events. If Áróra was to be entirely honest with herself, maybe she hadn't wanted them to reconcile completely. Maybe she wanted this rift between them to remain. It would make it easier for her to leave.

Yet now, as she looked at him staring straight ahead and gripping the steering wheel so tightly, she felt heavy-hearted, and it occurred to her for the first time that maybe she was wrong. Maybe this was a break-up. Her eyes filled with tears and the bleak landscape grew even more hazy, merging into an all-encompassing greyness.

Áróra wiped her eyes and straightened up in her seat. They

had reached the town of Reykjanesbær, and ahead was Keflavík Airport.

'I'll be back in the autumn,' she said, as much to herself as to him. 'And we'll keep in touch.'

'I know,' he said without looking at her. 'But it doesn't make this any easier.'

She laughed and gave a sniffle. 'No.'

She reached out her hand, and he took hold of it and clasped it tight. They drove like this, hand in hand, for the last stretch up to the airport. Daníel parked in the drop-off area and they sat for a while in silence. Then he placed his arm around her shoulders and pulled her close, and they embraced.

'Goodbye, Daníel,' she whispered into his ear.

'Don't say goodbye,' he whispered back. 'Say see you later.'

'See you later,' she said, and he kissed her several times on her cheek, ear, forehead, before letting her go.

Daníel climbed out of the car and took Áróra's suitcases out of the boot, while she gathered her hand luggage. They met a final time on the pavement, and she was relieved that after giving her a final fleeting hug, Daníel was back in his car when she burst into tears.

She watched him drive off, and when the car had vanished from view, she pulled a napkin from her pocket and dabbed her face.

'See you later,' she whispered to herself again as she walked into the airport terminal, not quite sure whether she was saying goodbye to Daníel, to Iceland or to her sister.

ACKNOWLEDGEMENTS

As I bring this series to a close, I want to express my gratitude to the many people who have travelled alongside Áróra and me on this journey.

First, my deepest thanks to my brilliant translators of the series, Quentin Bates and Lorenza Garcia, whose skill and sensitivity have carried Áróra's voice across languages and into new worlds of readers. Thanks also to my editor, West Camel, for his sharp eye and unfailing guidance, and to Karen Sullivan, my publisher, for her unwavering belief in this series from the very beginning.

I am also profoundly grateful to all those who have helped spread the word about these books: the tireless PR teams, the passionate bloggers, and everyone working behind the scenes to give Áróra her place in the world of crime fiction.

Most of all, I thank you, the readers, whose enthusiasm and support have meant everything. Your willingness to let Áróra into your lives has made her journey richer and more meaningful than I ever could have imagined.

Áróra has been my companion for many years, and saying goodbye to her is bittersweet. It warms my heart to know that you, too, will miss her. As we close the final chapter, I do so with immense gratitude – to her, to you, and for the stories we share.